THE LAST SNOW OF WINTER

IAN MUISE

Dreamspinner Press

Published by
Dreamspinner Press
4760 Preston Road
Suite 244-149
Frisco, TX 75034
http://www.dreamspinnerpress.com/

This is a work of fiction. Names, characters, places, and incidents either are the product of the author's imagination or are used fictitiously, and any resemblance to actual persons, living or dead, business establishments, events, or locales is entirely coincidental.

The Last Snow of Winter
Copyright © 2010 by Ian Muise

Cover Art by Reese Dante   http://www.reesedante.com

All rights reserved. No part of this book may be reproduced or transmitted in any form or by any means, electronic or mechanical, including photocopying, recording, or by any information storage and retrieval system without the written permission of the Publisher, except where permitted by law. To request permission and all other inquiries, contact Dreamspinner Press, 4760 Preston Road, Suite 244-149, Frisco, TX 75034
http://www.dreamspinnerpress.com/

ISBN: 978-1-61581-608-8

Printed in the United States of America
First Edition
October, 2010

eBook edition available
eBook ISBN: 978-1-61581-609-5

For Richard

Chapter 1

LOOKING up from the page he was skimming, Mark noticed it was getting late. He leafed through a few more pages of the dated text and considered whether it would do for what he had in mind. Of the nearly dozen books scrounged from the library shelves, only three showed promise for the project he was working on. He closed this last book and placed it with the other two he would be borrowing. Before leaving, he conscientiously deposited the rejects on a cart nearby for the library staff to return to their appropriate places.

There was a delay at the circulation desk as Mark attempted to check out his finds. One of the books wasn't even in the system. Though slightly impatient at the holdup, he was amused that this lonely little book was so out of date that no one had bothered to sign it out since before the library had installed the digital catalogue. *Perfect for my project*, he thought with satisfaction. The clerk, who Mark guessed was a fellow student, rambled away pleasantly while he entered the book's details into the computer and attached a new identification label to the inside cover. After ten minutes or so, he gave Mark a warm smile and passed the books over. Feeling self-conscious, though not certain why, Mark accepted them and tucked them into his bag. He was already out the door when it occurred to him that the clerk had been flirting. The realization stopped him in his tracks. *Could it be?* Mark was reluctant to trust his instincts, but the pieces all fit. *Why am I so dense?* He pushed himself back into motion and contemplated the huge blind spots in his social skills as he walked away.

Mark stepped into a large, echoing chamber that an architect might designate an atrium. Only a year earlier, the space had functioned as an entrance hall for the Beveridge Arts Centre. That was, of course, before the latest in a string of seemingly never-ending renovations rendered it redundant. Now it merely served as a connecting hub between the library and the two floors of the arts center. Arranged strategically around the room were several oversized bulletin boards. The maintenance staff had installed them in an effort to contain the ubiquitous advertisements, notices, and posters that seemed to appear daily. Despite their best efforts to maintain order, the chaos defied them. The material was now overwhelming the bulletin boards and escaping onto the brick walls and concrete columns nearby.

Mark crossed the empty room without surrendering to the visual din that called for his attention from every side. Loose papers rustled and waved at him lazily, stirred by the turbulence that trailed him. Ignoring the clutter, Mark instead listened to the noise his winter boots made against the tile floor. The familiar sound, altered and amplified by the open space and hard surfaces, returned as a clopping that reminded him fondly of horses. His eyes found his feet in an unconscious effort to connect with the sound. Countless footprints marred the floor beneath his boots, the dusty traces evidence of the traffic of the day. *Perhaps maintenance has given up on cleaning the floor until tomorrow,* Mark reasoned, *when there will be fewer people around to track in additional grime.*

Not far away, a pair of broad staircases led up or down a half-flight each. Mark descended to the lower level, taking the steps two at a time. Keeping to the center of the wide corridor, his long legs cut the distance to the exit like scissors. The corridor, like the atrium above, was wide by design to accommodate the periodic surge and flow of students, but it was evening now and the entire building appeared abandoned. Mark felt strangely remote passing through the too-large and abnormally quiet spaces.

Approaching the exit, a glimmer of movement where there should have been none caught the corner of his eye. A glance revealed the pale phantom drifting silently beside him to be his own image reflected in the glass that divided the Art Gallery from the corridor. The apparition jumped from pane to pane in a race to keep up, but it was the room beyond that held Mark's interest. The lights in the gallery were always on, even after hours. This evening the gallery was completely dark, transforming the windows into imperfect mirrors. *They must be changing the exhibit*, Mark mused. Satisfied with the observation, he marched on without slowing, his phantom-self left behind and forgotten.

Mark pushed past the double bank of doors that led out of the Beveridge Arts Centre. The B.A.C. was a sprawling, angular building that anchored one corner of the university grounds. This exit, pointed as it was directly toward the commercial core of Wolfville, acted almost like an airlock between the university and the town. It connected and separated the two communities. Due to its proximity to Main Street, these doors were one of the busiest access points to campus. For Mark it was just a convenient route home from the library.

Outside, the quiet street looked as deserted as the B.A.C. had been. Mark moved on at his usual quick pace. It was Friday evening, not late, but the sky was rapidly growing dark and streetlights were beginning to flicker to life in response to the spreading gloom. As spring approached, the daylight hours grew progressively longer, but night still came on fast this time of year.

Mark had been a student at the university for nearly four years now. In just a few weeks, he would complete the requirements for his undergraduate degree. A few papers and then final exams were all that stood in his way. Then, if all went well, he could start all over again at a new school. The steps of his future career were clearly laid out before him. Strangely, his future still seemed as impossibly distant as the new millennium, which was only eleven years away.

A term paper had kept him working late in the library. Normally he would have been home having supper by now, but he'd stayed back to do research. It had been quiet in the library, quieter than usual, even. Not surprising, really, as this was the last day of classes before the start of March break.

Crossing at the corner, barely checking to see if the way was clear, Mark started down Main Street. Settling in for the walk home, he shouldered his backpack and pulled up the hood of his coat to keep his ears warm. Though his hair was short enough to satisfy even the most demanding drill sergeant, he never wore a hat. In high school, Mark had worn his hair long. Over the last few years, the cut had gotten progressively shorter with each visit to the barber. Mark's mother was disappointed. He found it amusing that his mother preferred his hair longer. *Aren't mothers supposed to nag their sons into getting their hair cut?* Deep down, Mark reveled in being contrary to his parents, at least in the little things. Perhaps it made up for the big things.

There seemed to be no one else about this evening. If not for the lone, hooded individual marching purposefully down the center of the sidewalk, Wolfville might very well have been a ghost town. Most of the other students had fled earlier in the day, leaving town as soon as their classes ended, occasionally even before. Mark reflected on his decision to stay back a few extra days so he could finish a couple projects. His mother hadn't been happy when he'd called to let her know. Mark could tell by her tone that she was disappointed, but he was resolved not to give in. In the end, she told him she understood and thoughtfully cautioned him not to work too hard.

Mark had a friendly if somewhat politely distant relationship with his family. He would be the first to admit it was his own fault, but he didn't know how to repair the damage at this stage. Not wanting to brood over the dilemma again, he pushed the problem away for another time and forced himself to think about something else. He certainly didn't regret missing the overcrowded train back to Yarmouth. All the extra bodies would have made the trip even more tedious than usual. The Dayliner from Wolfville to his hometown typically took five hours. At Christmas, the last time Mark had made the trip, the train had seemed to stop every five minutes to let someone off. The journey had taken more than seven hours that night. *Yes*, Mark decided, *it's better to wait until Monday at least.* He could make a head start on some assignments and still have time to relax and see his friends and family.

Main Street, Wolfville, was part of the same continuous ribbon of asphalt that strung together all the little towns of the Annapolis Valley region of Nova Scotia. Mark glanced up the long street that would eventually take him to the tiny cottage he rented at the edge of town. Lamp poles now lit the street at regular intervals. The windows of shops and businesses in this part of town, however, were mostly dark, and there were few vehicles on the road. The quiet didn't bother him. Mark rather enjoyed the peacefulness of it all. At least that's what he told himself.

It had been a beautiful day. The sidewalks were bare of snow. What snow had been, had melted in the unseasonably warm temperatures. As the afternoon had waned and the temperature had dropped, the wet concrete had become treacherous with patches of black ice. Mark reduced his pace to navigate them safely.

Walking the sidewalk and cautiously avoiding the slippery patches engaged only part of his awareness. His mind was free to recall the incident in the library. The clerk seemed nice enough but wasn't really his type. *Was he really hitting on me?* Mark shook his head. *What's the point of worrying about it?* He then recalled the strange sensation he'd experienced when passing through the empty arts center. The B.A.C. was typically active with students. Tonight its corridors and lecture halls had been dimly lit and lifeless. Empty public spaces usually held a certain fascination for Mark. This evening was different. *Am I lonely?* Almost by reflex, Mark shied away from the question and concentrated more on placing his feet soundly. Now and then, one foot or the other threatened to slip him up, and he didn't want to end up on his ass again.

Minor slips and falls were a common enough occurrence during the valley winters. Snow started in November and often didn't retreat until April. Foot traffic packed down the snow, turning it to ice. Rock salt was of limited help in melting the ice, as the temperatures were often too low.

Mark recalled sitting in a requisite Statistics class during his first year at the university. Huge windows dominated one side of the lecture hall. Slightly bored by the subject, he let the view distract him. Through the windows, the bobbing heads and shoulders of pedestrians were visible as they passed by. He discovered that if you watched long enough, now and then a head would abruptly disappear from sight. The icy pathway had claimed yet another victim. A moment later, the head would reappear wearing a look of embarrassment. In the spirit of the class, it was tempting for Mark to treat his observations from the standpoint of statistical analysis. At what rate did people vanish? This was not to suggest he was unmoved by witnessing the misfortune of a stranger. None of the victims appeared seriously hurt by their fall; only their pride was injured. Just days before, he had fallen in nearly the same spot himself and understood their embarrassment firsthand. The reactions amused him, though. The unfortunate victims would pick themselves up, brush themselves off, and look around sheepishly to see if anyone had noticed the gaffe. Mark knew he had done the very same. Chalking the behavior up to human nature, he shook his head in amusement and reluctantly returned his attention to the lecture.

The maintenance staff who worked for the university did their best to keep the walkways and exterior steps as safe as possible. They obsessively cleared the snow and spread sand everywhere they could. Students quickly learned to clear out of the way when one of the sidewalk plows appeared in their path. In the spring, when all the snow and ice finally melted, the sand reappeared as a layer of dirt and grime, a reminder of the hard winter. Workers would dutifully sweep up the debris and truck it away. Mark wondered if they would use it again the next year. It seemed sensible to his way of thinking.

Walking this way, correcting for the little slips and occasional losses of footing, was becoming tiring. Mark could feel the pull and strain on the muscles of his legs and back. He had nearly reached the tiny park that separated the business core of downtown from the antique residences that lined the road out to the town limits. His place was just inside those limits. The walk usually took thirty minutes or so, but at the rate he was going, Mark knew it was going to be a while before he made it home.

Walking to and from school at least twice a day helped Mark maintain his well-muscled legs and trim waist. An impartial observer might describe him as lean, tall, dark, and even handsome. However, on those occasions when Mark received any such compliments, he shook them off self-deprecatingly. He joked that being a poor student made it easy to be thin as there was no extra money for food. Appearance-wise, Mark considered himself nothing special, perhaps even bordering on gangly.

THE LAST SNOW OF WINTER

Head down to keep an eye on his footing, Mark approached the end of a block of shops crowding the sidewalk. Just ahead, the structures stepped back from the street, making room for what the warmer weather would turn into attractively landscaped lawns and flowerbeds. As he stepped beyond the protection of the corner, a rushing impression of crashing into a wall surprised him. He quite literally didn't see what hit him. The impact forced the air out of his lungs. *I'm falling*, Mark realized. Just as the oddly calm thought occurred to him, there was a flash of light followed by nothingness.

"Hey, bud, are you okay?"

The voice that spoke the words was clear enough but gave Mark the impression of coming from a distance. He was having a little trouble sorting out what to say in response. He was aware that the ground was very hard. Opening his eyes, surprised to discover them closed, he asked the disembodied voice, "What happened?" Lying flat on his back, Mark looked up to find someone hulking over him. The streetlight overhead created an illusionary halo around the shadowy form. The light danced as he tried to focus on the stranger's face.

"I'm sorry. I didn't see you." After a moment's pause the shadow added, "You took a pretty good hit there. How do you feel?" The voice was friendly and carried a discernible coloring of concern.

"Um… I'm not sure," Mark replied quite honestly. He shifted in an effort to get up. The pain that shot through him was sudden and caused him to gasp sharply. Mark froze in response, holding himself still and closing his eyes against the wave of nausea that passed over him. The pain had come when he'd tried to move his right arm. When the nausea eased, he slowly and very cautiously tested the arm again. It felt heavy, and he couldn't seem to unbend it.

"Whoa, slow down there, bud!" A strong hand pressed down gently but insistently on the center of Mark's chest, keeping him in place. "How many fingers am I holding up?" The stranger held out his other hand for Mark to see.

Mark looked at the hand in front of his eyes and scowled without realizing it. "I'm not that bad off," he grunted in annoyance.

Unmoved by the tone of irritation, the large man insisted, "Yeah, yeah. How many?" He moved his hand in front of Mark's eyes again.

"Three. Your pinkie and thumb are folded over," Mark observed smartly.

The large man looked at his own hand and then grinned. He replied with a laugh, "Well, you can still see, anyway. That's good."

Mark blinked. He had to admit his vision was a little blurry. The light had stopped dancing, but his eyes watered. His head hurt, as did his arm, and there were other warning signals coming from here and there around his body, demanding his attention. None of it seemed too serious, though.

"Do you think you can sit up now?" the stranger enquired. The voice was so deep Mark could almost feel it resonate in his own chest.

"I think so," Mark replied tentatively. "Maybe."

"Take your time. Go slow. I can help." A strong arm slipped under Mark's left shoulder as he moved to get up. Slowly and gently, the stranger helped him. Coming to a sitting position, Mark's vision swam, and he felt sick again. His helper seemed to notice. "Close your eyes. Take your time." The voice was soothing. A big arm rested loosely over Mark's shoulder, the strong hand now in the middle of his back helping to steady him.

Even in pain, Mark couldn't help but tremble a little at the touch. It wasn't that often that anyone touched him, and Mark now recognized this man. "I know you," he said without thinking, regretting the words immediately.

"Yeah? Who am I?" the other asked suspiciously.

Feeling stupid now and wondering why he had said that aloud, Mark considered his options. While his helper wasn't a complete stranger, they certainly didn't know each other. They had never even spoken.

"You said you know who I am," the large man prodded.

THE LAST SNOW OF WINTER

It's too late to undo it now, Mark told himself. "You're Cliff Stevens," he observed in a flat voice. "You're on the football team. We have two classes together." The words seemed to tumble out. *Oh yes, that was smooth*, he thought self-consciously.

Cliff smiled good-naturedly. "I know you too," he said. "You're Mark Poole. You're the painter." There was only a slight hesitation before he added, "And you're gay… right?"

Experiencing a sudden sense of panic, Mark's mind raced. *Did he attack me? Is this some sort of weird variation on gay bashing?* His friend David had warned him ever since Mark had first come out to him that something like this would happen one day. Despite the apprehension he was feeling, Mark couldn't help but be amused by the intrusion of this odd thought.

Cliff seemed to read some of what was going through Mark's mind. "Hey, relax, bud. It's no big deal. I'm not going to leave you in a ditch or anything." He gave Mark a quick nod and what he hoped was a reassuring smile.

Mark hadn't seen the smile, but he could hear it in the tone of Cliff's voice. He forced himself to relax even though he felt exposed and a little frightened.

"How're you feeling?" Cliff asked.

What am I supposed to say to that? Cliff was still supporting and steadying him. Mark's vision had cleared, but his head was throbbing. His bum was cold from sitting on the ground, and there was definitely something wrong with his arm. He pulled it across his stomach and cradled it cautiously with his other arm. "I think there's something wrong with my arm. I can't move my elbow at all."

"How's your head? You hit it pretty hard when you fell," Cliff noted.

"It's been better." At least he didn't feel like he was going to throw up anymore. Mark was relieved. He was embarrassed enough without being sick in front of a stranger. *Well, that's dumb.* The intrusion of these strange random thoughts didn't alarm him too much. *Might as well be entertained by them, I guess.*

"Can you get up?" Cliff asked in a rumbling deep voice.

Brought back to the present, Mark answered, "I think so." He wasn't so sure but didn't want to seem weak in front of Cliff. Again, the odd pattern of his thinking struck him. *Maybe something came loose up there.*

Cliff was quick to support Mark as he attempted to pick himself up from the sidewalk. Mark felt almost lightheaded as Cliff lifted him easily. He was unsure if the dizziness he was experiencing was due to his head thumping, the motion of getting up, or the presence of the very beefy man holding him steady.

"When you're ready, I'm going to help you over to that bench." Cliff pointed to a bench at the edge of the tiny park up the street. It wasn't far. Mark didn't say anything but took a steadying breath and nodded in agreement. Pausing long enough for Cliff to collect Mark's backpack from the ground where it had fallen, the two men made their way out of the circle of light cast by the streetlamp overhead and started for the park. Cliff guided and watchfully assisted the smaller man. On reaching the bench, he turned Mark and gently directed him to a sitting position on the cold wooden slats. The air was crisp now, their breath clearly visible in trails of white vapor that vanished almost as quickly as it appeared.

Crouching at Mark's knees and leaning slightly forward, Cliff found Mark's eyes. On meeting Cliff Stevens for the first time, his imposing size made an immediate impression on people. At three hundred pounds of mostly muscle, he was well-suited to the sport he loved. The second thing a person noticed was his strikingly fierce eyes. Mark had never seen them from so close. They reminded him of the family dog, a Siberian husky named Blue. Those eyes seemed to see through you. Cliff's habit of meeting and holding a person's gaze when he addressed them heightened the effect. It felt almost aggressive. Over the last few months of classes, Mark had repeatedly observed people shying away from their intensity. He was startled out of his woolgathering when Cliff spoke.

"I want to check your head." Cliff's face was very close, well within Mark's usual personal boundaries. Before Mark could register

THE LAST SNOW OF WINTER

the intent of the words, Cliff rose and moved even closer to run his fingers gently over Mark's soft, closely cropped hair. Mark could feel the other man's breath in hot little blasts against his ear and neck. It sent shivers down his spine. "You have quite a bump there," Cliff said, indicating a spot behind and slightly above Mark's right ear. Again, there was a note of anxiety in his deep voice.

As he pulled away to look Mark in the face again, Cliff noticed a smudge of road grime that had dried on Mark's cheek. Without thinking, he brushed the chalky residue away with his thumb, his fingertips grazing the jaw line below the other man's ear. Looking for a moment at the face he was almost cupping with one hand, Cliff was completely astonished by what he was about to do. Without meaning to and unable to stop himself, he leaned in and kissed Mark softly on the lips.

Mark froze. The kiss lasted only an instant. It was feather-light. The barest pressure, and then it was over. At the end of it, Cliff pulled away so quickly it made Mark dizzy.

Cliff was standing now, not meeting Mark's eye as he said stiffly, "I'm going to run home and get my car. Don't move. I'll be right back. I'll take you over to the medical center so you can be checked out." Without another word, he turned and fled.

Mark was stunned. *What just happened? Is this some sort of practical joke?* His mind balked at understanding. He couldn't make sense of any of it. *Did he kiss me?* Warmth flooded his face. Mark knew he was blushing. He tried to clear his head. *Will he really come back?* Mark was suddenly aware that he was alone here. No one had driven or walked by the whole time since he'd opened his eyes to find Cliff crouching over him, or if someone had, Mark hadn't noticed. Looking up, he saw perfect little flakes of snow begin to float lazily down from the night sky.

Chapter 2

THERE were no sidewalks on the short side street that ran along one side of the park. Cliff ran as best as he could over the icy pavement. *What the hell were you doing? What were you thinking?* "Shit!" he spat out. He looked back over his shoulder. In the distance, he could just make out a dark shape on the bench he had left behind. A foot slipping unexpectedly on the frozen ground brought his attention back to where he was going. Cliff caught himself before falling and continued running.

A massively overgrown evergreen hedge marked the location of the converted house where Cliff had his apartment. As he turned into the driveway, he fished a set of keys out of his coat pocket. By chance, his downstairs neighbor was away and had taken her car with her. The driveway was large enough for two cars, but they had to park them in tandem, as the opening in the hedge was only wide enough for one. Living so close to campus, Cliff rarely bothered to drive. A gentleman both by nature and by conditioning, he usually let Karen have the spot closer to the street. Tonight, luckily, his car was free.

Taking a few deep breaths to steady his nerves and ease the pounding in his chest, Cliff unlocked and climbed into the car. It hesitated when he turned the key in the ignition. It had been days since he'd last started it. On the second try, the engine caught and roared to life. Cliff waited impatiently while the defogger worked to clear enough of the windshield to see out. Condensation had frosted over the inside of the glass when the temperature had changed. With bare hands, he rubbed at the stubborn frost. Unwilling to wait any longer, he hurriedly pulled the car out of the driveway and onto the street.

Cliff lived on the same side street adjacent to the little park. The park probably had a name, but everyone just referred to it as the duck pond. Cliff had been making a quick dash to the convenience store when he'd accidentally run into Mark at the corner and knocked him down.

"Shit! What were you thinking?" Cliff whispered the question as he recalled what he had done. He pictured Mark's gentle brown eyes and his beautifully shaped lower lip. The impulse to kiss that lip had overwhelmed him. Never before had he felt so compelled to an action in his life. Never before had he felt so out of control of himself. He was used to being in control. Gripping the steering wheel savagely, Cliff muttered "Shit" one last time. He sped back to the corner where he hoped Mark was still waiting. *Yes, there he is*, Cliff saw with relief. Having played football since high school, he had enough experience with injuries to know when to take them seriously. He also felt guilty for causing the injury in the first place.

Cliff left the car running with the heat and fan turned up as far as they would go. It would still take a few minutes for the car to warm up properly. The distance from his apartment to the corner with the park bench was only a few hundred meters. He felt a little sheepish as he approached Mark but purposely met his eye this time as he offered to help him up and to the car. Another man might have avoided making eye contact, feeling as embarrassed as he did, but Cliff's father had taught him to always look people in the eye.

Mark was almost surprised when a perfectly ordinary gray Volvo wagon pulled up to the curb not far from where he was sitting. In the back of his mind, he couldn't help the question: *A Volvo, seriously?* Shaking it off as unimportant, he watched the big football player walk up. He had practically convinced himself that Cliff wasn't coming back. Now that he had, Mark felt even more uncertain.

"Let me give you a hand," Cliff said. His voice came out a little stiffly. Mark didn't say anything in response but reached out with his good arm. Cliff easily pulled the smaller man up and guided him to the waiting car. After a few awkward and slightly painful maneuvers, Mark found himself safely positioned and strapped into the passenger seat of the very sensible car. Compared to the air outside, the interior of the car was warm. Mark didn't usually mind the weather, but it felt good to be out of the cold. Sitting there alone, unmoving and in pain, had chilled him deeply. It didn't help that his mind was still racing. Now that Cliff had actually come back, he didn't know if he was relieved or terrified.

After closing the passenger-side door, Cliff swiftly rounded to the driver's side of the car. Without a word, he put the car in gear and pulled away from the curb. Neither man said anything for several minutes. Cliff didn't even think to turn on the radio as they drove toward the medical center. Nothing interrupted the sound of the engine or the drone of tires on pavement as they moved through town. The tension sat between them like a physical presence. Cliff felt the need to do something to break it. With a lightness of tone he didn't feel, he said casually, "You okay over there? You're pretty quiet."

"Um... you kissed me." Mark hadn't meant to say it, but the memory kept replaying in his head.

Groaning inwardly, Cliff replied with a defeated sigh, "I was hoping we could just gloss over that."

Mark looked over to the other man. Not knowing what to think or say in response, he said nothing.

Glancing to the passenger side of the car before returning his eyes to the road, Cliff said, "I'm sorry. I don't know why I did it." That was true.

After a moment Mark replied, "I'm not complaining or anything. You sort of surprised me. That's never happened to me before."

"What? No strangers trying to take advantage of you in a weakened state?" Cliff kept his voice light, hoping to lift the mood. When he registered the words in his head, he felt stupid and closed his eyes a moment to block the memory.

"Not that I am aware of." Mark couldn't prevent the hint of bitterness that crept into his voice as he answered. If Cliff detected it, he didn't react.

An awkward silence fell over them for several minutes until Cliff gratefully pulled the car into the parking lot of the medical clinic. He quickly killed the engine, jumped out, and ran to the other side of the car to help Mark into the building.

The waiting area of the clinic was full of empty chairs. The lone person visible, a woman sitting behind the glass of a registration window, looked up from the novel she was reading. Wolfville didn't have its own hospital. The little towns that dotted their way through the Annapolis Valley were lightly populated and situated so close together that resources were shared between them. The nearest hospital was two towns over. Cliff would take Mark there if necessary, but the medical clinic was closer. Besides, he was familiar with the clinic. He had been going there for physiotherapy over the last year to help with a knee injury.

The receptionist or nurse, Mark couldn't tell from her uniform, leaned forward to bring her mouth closer to the opening in the glass partition. "Gentlemen, what seems to be the trouble?" she asked with a friendly smile.

Moving a little stiffly, Mark cautiously dropped into the chair opposite the receptionist. He wondered idly if she was annoyed at having her reading interrupted or relieved to have something to break up the monotony. Once seated, he noticed that Cliff had backed away slightly as if to give him privacy. "I had a little fall," he explained to the woman. "My right elbow won't straighten out."

From over Mark's shoulder, Cliff added in a clear voice, "I think he broke the arm, and he hit his head too. There's quite a bump. He looked a little pale earlier, and I think he blacked out for a few seconds when he fell." The words sounded clinical, but Mark believed he could hear that tone of concern again. It made him blush, though he couldn't explain why even to himself.

After jotting down Mark's health card number and other relevant information, the receptionist said, "I'll get someone to take your vitals and let the doctor on duty know you're here. Just take a seat right over there. It should only be a few minutes." She indicated a neat row of identical chairs lined up near a plain door that Mark assumed led to the examination area.

A helping hand was on Mark's good elbow when he got up to change seats. Mark was not very touchy-feely as a rule. A few of his friends were more tactile, and he did what he could to accommodate them, but he didn't encourage casual physical contact. Tonight, however, Mark found the occasional touches from the burly football player to be quite exciting. Though now that he considered it, he could feel his ears go hot again.

Cliff didn't seem to notice Mark's blush. At least, he didn't comment on it. They each took a seat in one of the worn vinyl waiting room chairs. Cliff left an empty chair between them. It didn't feel like a slight to Mark. Even with the empty seat between them, their shoulders were still almost touching.

Under the harsh fluorescent lights of the waiting room, Mark noticed for the first time the spatters of dried salt and dirt on the leg of Cliff's jeans and the sleeve of his coat. Realizing the other man must have fallen, too, he asked with concern, "Did you fall? When I did, I mean. You have salt stains all over your side."

Cliff looked down to where Mark was indicating with his eyes. "Yeah, I fell too." He shrugged. "Don't worry about it. I take tackles all the time, though not usually on the street." He winked and then added, "You have salt and dirt all over your backside too."

The door beside them opened abruptly, causing both men to start. A woman stepped into the waiting room, quickly looked them over, turned to Mark and addressed him by name. She was very short, perhaps a head and a half shorter than Mark. She had tight black curls on her head and a slightly playful look to her face. She was obviously young. Mark liked her instantly.

"I'm Dr. Park. I would offer to shake your hand, but I do not think you would appreciate it right now. Okay, let's see how bad things are. Are you guys together?" She asked the question businesslike, looking from one baffled face to the other. Not waiting for an answer, she nodded to Cliff and added, "You might as well come too." She then turned on her heel and walked back the way she had come. The doctor had spoken quickly the whole time, giving them no opportunity to respond. They followed her obediently.

As they walked into a small exam room, the doctor turned to Cliff and demanded, "Did you do this to him? You boys should be more careful when you're playing around." The smile belied the tease, but Mark could feel his ears go hot again. He wasn't sure why everything seemed to be making him blush this evening. It left him feeling terribly exposed.

"It was an accident, Doctor," Cliff replied sheepishly.

"I should hope so." The doctor got to work with a manner of quiet efficiency. "We'll need an X-ray," she said seriously. "First I have some questions."

Chapter 3

THE X-ray was an ordeal. In order to get the best images, the technician instructed Mark to twist and hold his aching arm in a number of awkward and painful positions. Following directions as best he could, Mark used up his last reserves of energy. It was a relief when the procedure was finally over, and the technician sent him back to the exam room where Cliff was waiting. Shivering without being aware of it, Mark entered the room feeling worn out. He wanted to go home. The pain was terrible. He felt cold and tired.

When Mark stepped through the door, Cliff appraised his condition openly with concern. He stood and put his arm around the smaller man's shoulders, guiding him to the chair he had just vacated. He felt Mark relax instinctively into the warmth of his body. The shivering eased. Shocked by the strong protective feelings he had for this man beside him, Cliff told himself it was just because he felt guilty for injuring him and nothing more. He was afraid it was a lie.

When the doctor entered the room some minutes later, she held a set of X-rays in one hand and a little paper cup in the other. "I want you to take these," she said. She held out the cup, which held two white pills. "It will help with the pain and swelling. There is water over there if you need it."

The doctor watched as Cliff immediately intercepted the cup, palmed the pills, and quickly stepped to the sink to fill the cup with water. He returned, handing first the pills and then the water to Mark.

Once Mark had swallowed the pills, Dr. Park snapped one of the X-rays into a light box mounted on the wall and flipped the switch. The fluorescent light flickered coolly and then brightened to reveal an image. Mark knew enough anatomy to recognize what he was seeing. The doctor pointed out a fine line crossing one of the bones. "You have a radial head fracture... here," she said, partly facing the wall. "Luckily the bones are undisplaced." She looked back at Mark and Cliff. "It looks good. I don't think you will need surgery, but we will know more in a few days."

"Why doesn't it move?" Mark asked, looking away from the X-ray to the doctor.

"It is your body's way of avoiding pain. The break released fluid into the joint. I don't think we will put a cast on it for now. However, I want you to wear a sling. If everything goes well, you will need to start physiotherapy soon so we can restore normal movement." After a moment of thought, the doctor added, "I am a little concerned about the bump to your head. How do you feel about a night at the hospital, just for observation?" The look Mark gave her must have conveyed what he thought of the idea. She said with a laugh, "That's what I figured."

"I can keep an eye on him," Cliff volunteered quietly, not looking at Mark.

Accepting that without comment, Dr. Park advised, "Take Tylenol for the pain and swelling, nothing stronger because of the head injury. Here's a sling." She pulled a plastic-wrapped package from one of the cupboards beside the sink and helped Mark put it on and adjust it. She continued with instructions and directions. Mark wasn't following it all. The doctor began directing more of the conversation toward Cliff. The medication wasn't the sort to have any effect on Mark's concentration, but the ordeal of the evening had been a strain. He was exhausted.

"I want to see you tomorrow at 6:00 p.m.," Dr. Park said, raising her voice and directing her attention to Mark again. "Just to see how things are going. Get rest, take it easy, keep your arm still... and no more roughhousing, you two," she said finally with a small smile, pointing to each of them in turn.

Blushing yet again, Mark attempted unsuccessfully to struggle into his coat. He had removed it earlier easily enough but now had no idea how he would get it back on over the sling. With Cliff's help, he slipped his good arm into a sleeve and draped the open coat over the other shoulder.

Once they reached the main doors, Cliff said, "You wait here, I'll get the car ready." He was off without waiting for an answer. Mark watched him go. He wondered why the guy was helping. *The fall was an accident, after all.* Even as he considered it, Mark was grateful for the assistance.

Snow must have been falling the whole time they'd been in the clinic. A light dusting of fluffy flakes covered the ground. Cliff swept the windows of the car clear with his arm. He knew he really should invest in a brush and scraper, but he never thought about it when he had the opportunity. When the car windows were relatively clear and the engine was started, he ran back to where Mark was waiting just inside the door of the clinic.

After Cliff had gotten Mark safely settled in the car and had strapped himself in, too, he realized he hadn't given thought to what would happen next. He could see Mark shivering again. The little guy seemed to be going into a mild state of shock. "Whereabouts do you live?" he asked.

"Out at Roselawn Cottages, at the other end of town," Mark explained.

"Right." Cliff knew the place. Roselawn was a motel and cottages business during the summer, but the owner rented to students in the off-season. "The doctor thinks you should have someone with you for the next few hours anyway, just in case your head injury is more serious than it seems. Do you have a roommate or anyone?" Cliff could feel himself tense as he asked the question. It surprised him. *After all, what is it to me if Mark has a boyfriend at home?*

"My roommate went home for March break earlier today. There isn't anyone else," Mark answered simply.

Slightly uncomfortable at the relief he felt in hearing Mark's answer, Cliff went on. "I can stay for a while to keep an eye on you. Oh, you should give me your number now in case I forget to ask later." He began fumbling for a notepad and pen he kept in the center console.

"Number? Oh, I don't have a phone," Mark replied when he realized what Cliff was asking. After looking into the possibility, Mark and his roommate had decided it was too difficult to hook up a phone for just eight months. Besides, it wasn't like they really needed it.

"No phone! What if something happens to you?" Cliff could tell he was overreacting but seemed to be a bystander watching the performance from the sidelines.

"There's a payphone at the main building." Mark was surprised at Cliff's clear show of alarm. It wasn't that unusual not to have a phone. Many students didn't bother with the expense, and the phone company certainly didn't make it easy for them to get one.

"How is that going to help you if you're lying unconscious on the floor?" The protective feelings he was experiencing for someone he barely knew astonished Cliff.

Mark was tempted to laugh at how seriously Cliff was taking this. When he turned to face Cliff though, he sobered and kept his mouth closed. He couldn't suppress the little smile.

Seeing the smile, Cliff growled, "I know, you think I'm blowing things out of proportion. I'm just concerned."

"Thank you," Mark said quietly. It was flattering that this big bear of a man cared.

Disarmed, Cliff sighed. It was all very strange. He wasn't used to feeling this way. He changed the subject by asking, "You hungry?"

Surprised at the abrupt change in direction, Mark took a few seconds to reply. "Yeah, I haven't eaten yet. I'm really tired though. I think I need to lie down for a bit."

"Why don't I take you to my place?" Cliff then stressed, "Where I have an actual working telephone. You know, to call the paramedics in case you die or something. I can get us a bite to eat. You can rest, and I can keep an eye on you." Cliff assured himself it was a perfectly logical and reasonable offer.

"I don't want to be an inconvenience," Mark explained and then continued semi-seriously, "Especially if I am going to die and all." He laughed out loud now.

"You shit." Cliff laughed too. He reached over intending to pinch Mark's thigh playfully, stopping himself just as the other man pulled away in reaction to the move.

The reflex action caused Mark to wince in pain. He had forgotten his arm. "No roughhousing, remember?" Mark relaxed once he saw that Cliff wasn't making any suspicious moves. For a brief but terrifying moment, he had been afraid the brute was going to tickle him.

As he pulled out of the parking lot and turned the car back toward town, Cliff was pleased to see Mark gingerly rest his head on the headrest and close his eyes. Mark, apparently asleep, didn't say another word during the drive. It gave Cliff time to wonder at how comfortable he felt with the little guy. *Not that he's all that little*, Cliff corrected after sizing him up discreetly. Mark was perhaps an inch or two shorter than he was, Cliff figured. *He's a six-footer, anyway.* It amazed Cliff that his well-crafted defenses were completely thrown by this guy. Cliff wasn't ready to sort out why just now. He just needed to keep himself under control.

Chapter 4

THE apartment Cliff rented had been his home for the last three years. It made up what had once been the upper floor of a single-family dwelling. Like many other large houses in Wolfville, its owner had converted it into apartments to accommodate and cash in on the student population from the university. It was a small place but comfortable. The kitchen was tiny, but the bathroom was huge. Because of his size, Cliff appreciated the large bathroom.

When the lulling motion of the car stopped, Mark woke disoriented. He didn't recognize the house he saw through the windshield of the car. It took a few moments to remember that Cliff had taken him to his place. *This must be it.* He moved to open the car door. The familiar action caused him to draw in a sharp breath and grunt in pain. He had forgotten about his arm again.

Cliff caught the sound and worked out the cause. "Wait a minute," he said, both amused and slightly exasperated. He exited the car and walked around to the passenger side to help Mark out of the car.

An exposed wooden staircase led to the entrance of the second-story apartment. The snow that had accumulated on the steps crunched under the tread of their boots. Cliff unlocked the door and guided Mark inside. He then grabbed a broom, stepped back outside, and said he would just be a minute. The door closed behind him.

Mark hadn't known what to expect on entering. *What does a jock's place look like, anyway?* He had no experience to draw on for comparison. Looking around, it was all very ordinary. There was the typical mismatched furniture, all slightly worn and dated, probably castoffs retired from the family home or items picked up at yard sales. It didn't look that much different from Mark's own place. Except that while Mark's landlord didn't allow tenants to make holes in the walls, Mark had compromised by temporarily replacing the generic artwork that came with the furnished cottage with his own paintings. He'd used the very same nails. Otherwise, the boring off-white walls would have been too depressing for him. *Cliff's landlord must have a similar rule,* Mark thought, *or maybe the man doesn't care for decoration.* In either case, the walls were completely bare. On the other hand, the upper portion of several of the walls sloped into the low roofline. That definitely made it harder to display things on them. Mark suspended judgment for now and continued looking around.

This was obviously the living room. Light came from a couple of table lamps. A pair of low bookcases dominated one side of the room, filled to overflowing with what Mark took to be textbooks. Opposite the bookcases was an ugly, floral-print sofa disguised by a heavy wool blanket. The overall effect was that the apartment felt warm and homey, even if the walls were a bit bare.

Having swept the stairs clear of snow, Cliff returned to the apartment. His glasses fogged instantly in the warm air. Snowflakes were melting on the exposed skin of his shaved head. Unable to see clearly, it took Cliff a moment to realize that Mark hadn't moved since Cliff had left him. He hadn't even taken off his heavy outer clothes. "Make yourself at home," he said. Unasked, he helped Mark out of his coat.

Removing his winter boots took a little careful planning, but Mark managed to get them untied and off without assistance. He stepped away from the door to give his host more room to maneuver in removing his own things.

Cliff felt a little self-conscious as he watched Mark glance around his living room. It was rare that he had anyone in here. It wasn't like he was antisocial or anything, just a little private. As he watched, Mark twisted in an apparent effort to gauge how dirty the backs of his pant legs were. Cliff guessed the reasoning behind the action and offered,

"Don't worry about the furniture. Or if you like, I can lend you something to wear. It'll be a little big on you." He shrugged.

"Ah, sure, thanks." Mark didn't want to get the furniture dirty. Then he said, "But I really need to use your bathroom."

"Right through there." Cliff indicated a door over his shoulder with his thumb. "Let me grab you something to change into first." He disappeared through a doorway into a darkened room. A moment later, he returned and handed Mark a pair of fleece gym shorts. "They'll be big on you, but they have a tie at the waist. That should help."

Cliff's prediction had been correct. The shorts were far too big. At least the elastic was keeping them up. Mark was relieved. He hadn't been able to do anything with the drawstring and was reluctant to ask for help. He caught himself in the mirror. It felt very odd to be wearing someone else's clothes. Mark was also uneasy about being in a stranger's home. Deciding he had been in the bathroom long enough, he took a deep breath, forced himself to inefficiently wash his one free hand, and then stepped out of the bathroom.

Mark found Cliff straightening the living room. It hadn't been that messy to begin with, but Cliff was busy collecting and stacking all the books and papers that had covered the surface of the coffee table when they'd come in. Mark noticed his coat hanging next to Cliff's on a hook by the door, and there were his boots lined up on the mat. *Relax*, he told himself. He placed his clumsily folded jeans over the back of a chair. He could see that Cliff had changed as well. His host was now wearing sweatpants and a well-broken-in T-shirt. The thin and faded cotton was barely able to contain Cliff's wide shoulders and deep chest. The effect impressed Mark. He liked that Cliff looked more Highland strongman than professional bodybuilder. The sweatpants were another story. Mark's friend David insisted that sweatpants weren't appropriate for polite society. Noticing the sizable and slightly indecent bulge in Cliff's pants, Mark had to agree that maybe David was right. Not that he was going to complain. But just to be respectful, he carefully kept his gaze away from that general area. He suspected that Cliff wasn't wearing anything underneath the fleece pants.

"Do you want to lie down?" Cliff asked when he noticed that Mark had returned from the bathroom.

Mark considered the offer. There was no question it was tempting. His head felt heavy, but he was confident he wouldn't be able to rest right now. *Maybe you should have asked him to take you home.*

Sensing the hesitation, Cliff offered, "You can use the couch or my bed if you like."

"I think I'll just sit here for a while," Mark replied, indicating the couch.

"Do you eat pizza?" Cliff enquired, changing the subject in an effort to make his guest and himself more comfortable.

"Ah… yes." Mark nodded.

"I'll call for delivery," Cliff said. "Any preferences?"

"Preferences?" Distracted by his own discomfort, the question confused Mark.

"Yeah, you know… toppings." Cliff mimed a sprinkling motion with his fingers.

Understanding, Mark replied, "Oh, anything's good," and then clarified, "except olives… and fishies." Mark was smiling as he said it.

"Fishies?" Cliff asked, incredulous, looking at the man sitting on his couch.

"Anchovies." Mark wrinkled his nose at the idea.

"Right! No fishies." Amused, Cliff turned away and picked up the phone. After ordering the pizza and hanging up the receiver, Cliff turned back to face his guest. "Twenty minutes," he said, indicating the time that would pass before their food would arrive. He wondered what he should do next. He considered putting on some music but was afraid that would make it feel too much like a date. *Why is this so hard?* Not knowing what else to do, he took a seat at the other end of the couch. The minutes ticked by without a word passing between them.

Occupied by his own nervousness, Mark didn't notice Cliff's unease. Afraid he was being a poor guest, he decided to make the most of the situation and said conversationally, "I like your place."

"Thanks."

"I wasn't sure what to expect," Mark continued.

"What do you mean? Did you think I lived in a barn?" Cliff said with a laugh.

"No, I've just never been in a football player's apartment before." Mark hadn't meant to offend.

"What is that supposed to mean? Just because I play football doesn't mean I'm any different than you." Cliff's voice had an edge to it now.

This wasn't going at all like Mark intended. "I'm sorry. I didn't mean any insult. It's just… well, I was never in the popular crowd at school. It always seemed like they lived different lives somehow," Mark explained lamely.

"You mean the jocks?" Cliff turned to Mark and raised his brows as he asked the question.

"If I say yes, am I going to end up in that ditch somewhere?" Mark faced Cliff and assumed a look of exaggerated timidity.

Am I overreacting? After a few seconds of quiet thought, Cliff replied by observing, "It wasn't all that great on the inside either."

Mark considered that. "I guess I was too wrapped up in my own problems at the time to give it any thought."

Cliff made an effort to be less defensive. "What problems?" Despite the misunderstanding, he was grateful to have a break from the uncomfortable silence, and he was genuinely interested.

"Oh, normal teenage stuff: hormones, mood swings, and coming to terms with being gay." Mark waited several seconds before asking, "How did you know I was gay?" Though Mark never pretended or tried to mislead people, he wasn't really open about his sexuality. He certainly wouldn't describe himself as out.

"I was only guessing," Cliff admitted. "I noticed you watching me in class." His tone was even and his expression unreadable.

"Oh." Mark felt nervous. He was relieved that Cliff didn't seem to be offended. "I didn't mean to...." He trailed off, uncertain what to say.

"It's okay. It puzzled me at first. You didn't seem intimidated by me. Most people are, at first." In fact, Cliff had to admit that he intimidated most people even after they knew him. *If they bother to get to know you at all*, he amended grimly.

"I think you want them to be," Mark said, surprising even himself. *Has my brain stopped working completely?* He watched Cliff apprehensively for his reaction.

Taken aback, Cliff was quiet for a full minute before asking evenly, "Why do you say that?"

"I didn't say that right. Let me see if I can explain better." Mark paused to collect his thoughts before continuing. He didn't want to offend his host any more than he apparently already had. Speaking slowly, he began with, "You have this very fierce persona that you project. It intimidates people. But it seems to me that it isn't native to your personality. It feels like it's imposed on your original nature from outside. I can't explain why I feel that way." Mark really couldn't. It was just a feeling he got.

Cliff didn't respond.

"Could you at least leave me in a ditch near my place?" Mark hoped the joke would lighten the mood.

"Why are you so worried about being beaten up and left in a ditch?" Cliff asked irritably, happy to change the subject.

A loud rap sounded at the door. As Cliff got up to answer the knock, Mark was relieved to have escaped even temporarily from this disaster of a conversation.

A few minutes later, Cliff placed the pizza box on the coffee table in front of Mark. He went to the kitchen to get plates. "What would you like to drink? I have beer, water, pop...."

"Whatever you're having?" Mark replied.

Cliff returned with two plates and two cold bottles of beer. He hesitated a moment at the propriety of giving alcohol to someone who might have a head injury. *Surely one beer won't make a difference.* To cover the hesitation, he asked, "You don't like to make decisions?" Handing a plate over and setting the bottles down, he resumed his seat on the couch and pulled a slice of pizza from the box. Following his host, Mark did the same. He performed the task a little clumsily, trying to get the slice on a plate one-handed. Cliff noticed the effort and opened both bottles preemptively to save his guest the trouble.

"Thank you," Mark said in response to the thoughtful gesture. He now considered the question of making decisions. "Other people have said the same to me. It's a habit, I guess." He took a bite and thought it over a little more. Mark finally answered, "I guess I just don't want to be a bother. It's good Catholic training, you know." In explanation, he confessed, "I went to Catholic schools for a while."

"You're Catholic?" Cliff was surprised. Then he was afraid his question had sounded rude.

"No, I've reformed." Mark was obviously unembarrassed by the subject.

This guy was not at all what Cliff had expected. The more he learned about him, the more he wanted to know. "Reformed into what?" he asked.

"Non-Catholic," Mark replied immediately with a little laugh and a mischievous grin.

Putting the topic aside for another time, Cliff decided to go back to the question he'd asked earlier. "So you were going to tell me why you're so worried about getting left in a ditch. You're a big enough guy. I'm sure you can take care of yourself."

Thinking about the question while chewing a bite of pizza, Mark swallowed and said, "David, a friend of mine, is always worried I'm going to be the victim of gay-bashing."

"Why?" Cliff was shocked. *What kind of friend is that?*

"He's just worried about me. It happens." Mark shrugged. "Maybe he thinks I'm too naive. Anyway, as far as being able to take care of myself, I don't think it matters how big you are if a couple guys jump you when you aren't expecting it." It was true, but Mark didn't spend a lot of time worrying about it.

Cliff couldn't argue with that. They ate in silence for a few bites.

"On the other hand, if I was the size of a moose like you, maybe I would be braver," Mark observed casually.

"You just called me a moose. That could be brave... or dangerous." Cliff lowered his voice to imitate a menacing growl.

Mark was certain that Cliff hadn't been insulted by his comment, but he qualified his previous statement by saying, "Technically I said you were the size of a moose, not an actual moose. If that makes it any better. In any case, size doesn't make you brave. How does it go? Bravery isn't a matter of not being afraid. It's the manner in which you face your fears."

"So why did you say that you might be braver if you were as big as me?" Cliff was intrigued by Mark's way of looking at things.

"Oh, I guess I felt scrawny as a kid. I always wanted to look more like you. I know better now. It wouldn't matter what I looked like." Mark knew that was true. "I look around and see blonds who want to be brunettes and vice versa. But a part of me still wonders if it would be easier if... or would I be more accepted if... whatever." Mark added lightly, "Low self-esteem is the price you pay for surviving growing up gay."

"I like the way you look." The unguarded assertion astonished Cliff. He'd responded again without thinking. *How does this little guy get around my defenses so easily?*

Not sure how to take Cliff's comment, Mark took another bite of pizza instead.

"I think you are brave," Cliff said, looking at his plate. "I have a pretty good idea of how much pain you must be in, and you're sitting here with me and not saying a word about it."

"That's not brave," Mark said, looking down to his arm. "It hurts. But it won't help to bother you about it."

Cliff didn't agree. "Sometimes sharing can help. Don't you ever let people help you?" He wanted to help.

"I'm not very good at that. I don't...."

Already knowing what Mark was about to say, Cliff finished the sentence for him. "I know, I know, you don't want to be a bother."

Mark sighed.

"Well I'm bigger than you, and I'm going to help you whether you like it or not. And there's nothing you can do about it." Cliff nodded his head once firmly to back up the declaration.

Amused, Mark really didn't know how to take it. He wished it meant one thing but was sure it didn't. His mind teased: *But then he did kiss you.* Mark had almost forgotten. He yawned noisily, suddenly feeling very tired.

Noticing the yawn, Cliff said, "It's late, and you're tired. You're going to stay here tonight so I can keep an eye on you. Off to bed." Cliff pointed to the doorway where he had gone to get the shorts earlier.

Mark looked to the door and asked uncertainly, "What about you?"

"I can sleep on the couch."

"I can't take your bed! This is your home." Mark was nearly indignant. He was trying his best to accept this stranger's help graciously, but taking his bed seemed too much.

"You can't sleep out here with that arm. If we share the bed, I'll keep you up, or I'll roll over and squash you by accident. Remember, I'm bigger than you." Cliff crossed his arms to fend off further argument.

He certainly was an impressive sight. With his broad shoulders, shaved head, sexy russet-colored goatee, and striking blue eyes, Mark was sure Cliff could convince him to do almost anything. However,

Mark was naturally stubborn. "You won't even fit on the couch. Together, or I walk home."

"You shit! You're just trying to get me into bed." Cliff was smiling broadly. He looked at the smaller man. Oh yes, he didn't doubt Mark would walk out. He could easily sense the stubbornness. Cliff allowed himself to study Mark for a moment. He appeared lean and graceful to Cliff's eye. His skin still carried a little color from the sun despite the season. His hair and eyes were dark. Overall, there was something almost brooding about him. Cliff liked what he saw. He also liked what he knew of the man inside. "You win. We share the bed. If anyone asks, I just hope you'll protect my virtue."

"Well, as you've already pointed out, you're bigger than me, and I'm wounded. I'm pretty sure your virtue is safe." Mark made the statement wearing an air of innocence.

"Humph. Come on then." Cliff led the way to the bedroom. He entered and crossed the dark room to click on a lamp by the bed. "I warn you now, I sprawl." He walked past Mark, who was standing just inside the doorway. "You get comfy. I'll clean up a bit and put the leftovers away."

The whole time Cliff was packing the pizza away in the fridge and rinsing the plates, he kept telling himself to calm down. He considered letting Mark fall asleep and spending the night on the couch. Sure, the guy would give him hell in the morning, but it would be easier on his nerves. *Yeah, that would be brave. No, we're going to do this.* When Cliff finally returned to the bedroom, it was to find Mark still dressed and sitting on the edge of the bed nearest the door.

"I didn't know if you preferred to sleep on a particular side." Mark looked up at the man filling the doorway, feeling slightly pathetic. "And I couldn't get my shirt off."

Cliff felt more of his defenses slipping away, and this time he didn't care as much. "Let me help you." The two men struggled to get Mark's T-shirt over his head without causing him too much discomfort.

"Do you want to sleep with the sling on?" Cliff asked.

"I think I better." Mark groaned, "Oh, this is going to be so much fun."

"Do you need help getting your shorts off?" Cliff enquired playfully.

"Thanks, I'll manage." Mark's face felt hot again.

It was then that Cliff remembered he had removed his underwear when he'd changed out of his dirty jeans earlier.

Mark looked up at the man standing frozen beside him. "What's wrong?"

"I'm not wearing underwear," Cliff answered automatically, and then wondered why he had said that out loud instead of making something up.

"I thought so." Mark smiled knowingly.

"What?" Cliff turned to look at him, dumbfounded.

"Hey, I'm not the one going around without underwear. I'm allowed to notice." Seeing Cliff go red, Mark added, "I only looked once." Then thinking perhaps he had gone too far, he sobered, "I'm sorry. Are you okay with all this?"

Sure, he was okay. Cliff had been naked around other guys in the locker room all the time. *It's no big deal*, he told himself. He didn't believe it. "I usually sleep nude. I wasn't thinking when I changed," Cliff explained.

"I usually sleep in the nude too. It's no big deal." Mark shrugged.

Forcing himself to move, Cliff pulled his shirt over his head in one motion. Then he pushed his pants down and stepped out of them. "Your turn," he addressed Mark, facing him boldly.

Stunned at what he was seeing, Mark hesitated a moment before struggling out of the borrowed shorts and slipping off his underwear.

"Should I help?" Cliff asked teasingly, watching from where he had moved to the other side of the bed.

"No!" Mark finally pulled off his socks and turned back to see Cliff standing there naked, still watching him.

"Now we're even." Cliff jumped into bed and adjusted the covers.

Mark did the same, blushing furiously.

"Night." Cliff reached over, placed his glasses on the night table, and turned off the lamp.

Chapter 5

IT WASN'T completely dark in the bedroom. Light from the street cast irregular patterns on the wall and ceiling through gaps between the blind and window. Lying on his back with his injured arm across his chest, Mark watched the unfamiliar patterns for what seemed like hours. He had no idea how much time had passed since Cliff had turned out the light. Used to sleeping on his side, he felt uncomfortable this way. Mark often found it difficult to sleep in a strange bed, but tonight, listening to the sound of a relative stranger breathing beside him, it was impossible.

Mark recalled a mental image of a naked Cliff standing by the bed. Oh yes, the massive football player looked better than Mark could have ever imagined. Cliff's chest was thickly furred. Just the thought of it made Mark itch to feel it under his hands. *That's dangerous*, he cautioned himself. He could feel his cock stir in response to the idea. *But he kissed you*, his brain teased. *Oh, what am I doing here? Why am I torturing myself? A guy like Cliff would never want to be with someone like me.*

"You're awake." The sleepy voice broke into Mark's thoughts.

Mark hadn't heard the change in Cliff's breathing and was startled to find him awake. "Sorry, did I wake you?"

"No. Are you okay?" Concern was perceptible in Cliff's voice despite the obvious drowsiness.

"It's hard to get comfortable, but I'm okay. I guess I was thinking too much to sleep," Mark answered honestly.

Shifting onto an elbow and turning to face Mark's side of the bed, Cliff asked, "Thinking about what?" He sounded more alert now.

What do I say? "Well, wondering why I'm here lying in bed with a stranger." Mark realized he was too sore and too tired to apply the usual filters to his speaking. *Very dangerous!*

"Is that all?" Cliff unsuccessfully stifled a yawn.

"No." Mark knew he should just stop talking now but continued anyway. "I was wondering... if I would ever find someone like you for my own. Or would I just be lonely forever." Oh, that sounded so pathetic to his ears. Cliff would probably despise him.

"I wonder about stuff like that too. Maybe everyone does." Cliff's voice sounded sleepy again.

Mark wanted to ask "Why did you kiss me? What did it mean?" He couldn't make the words come out.

"Go to sleep. We can talk about it in the morning." Cliff shifted toward the other man, reached out, and rubbed Mark's stomach lightly under the covers.

It was far too easy to interpret the gesture as a sign of affection. Mark pushed his head back into the pillow. He rolled his eyes up to the ceiling as if pleading for a God he wasn't even sure existed to take pity and send him some... sign. No sign came. Mark hadn't really expected one. He turned his head to watch Cliff, who was apparently sleeping again. They could be friends, Mark realized. He knew they could. That should be enough. Mark closed his eyes and listened to the rhythm of Cliff's breathing.

Chapter 6

THE room was aglow with warm yellow light. The flimsy blind at the window kept out the direct sunlight but did little to keep the room dark. Cliff never minded. He usually got up early anyway. As he became more alert, he noticed his hand was resting on Mark's belly just below Mark's injured arm. Mark was still sleeping. It was strange to be sharing a bed.

Cliff remembered waking up through the night and finding Mark unable to sleep. He was pleased to see him resting now. He watched his face as he slept. Fine lashes, skin a warm brown tint in the amber light, a closely trimmed beard that Cliff knew from experience was wiry to the touch. Cliff's gaze wandered to Mark's full lips. A picture of himself biting that bottom lip sprang into his head unbidden. Awareness of his body's reaction to this train of thought washed over Cliff suddenly. The arousal frightened him. *You can't do this. You've worked so hard. You can't throw it all away.* Cliff carefully pulled his hand away and slipped off the mattress as lightly as he could. On the floor near the bed were the pants and T-shirt he'd worn the evening before. He picked them up and padded quietly to the door. Stopping before leaving the room, he looked back once to watch Mark still sleeping peacefully.

In the bathroom with the door closed, Cliff turned on the lights and squinted at himself in the mirror. Unhappy, he turned his back on the reflection and faced the opposite wall instead. He brought his hand up to rub his eyes, dropping his head slightly. Cliff's brain seemed to be waging war with itself inside his skull. One side argued, *You can't do this. It's too risky, and it's not worth it,* while another part whispered, *He likes you, and he wants you. You know he does. He would let you. He would have you. No one has to know.* "No!" That silenced the argument. Cliff knew he couldn't act on these feelings. He reached over and opened the flow of water in the shower.

Mark woke in a strange bed. It took a few minutes to pull all the drifting pieces of consciousness together. The room glowed cheerfully but not so brightly that he couldn't roll over and go back to sleep. The sound of water running nearby helped to push the tempting idea away. This was Cliff's bed. He needed to get up so he could go home and get out of the guy's way. *Cliff will want to be clear of me by now. Straight guys don't share their bed with other guys. Do they?* Mark really didn't know. He usually didn't let people get that close. No, he was sure Cliff would be ready to see him gone. He hadn't died, after all. Remembering, Mark smiled to himself and then reviewed the events of the night before. He immediately felt embarrassed at how he had exposed himself, both emotionally and physically. *What was I thinking? How am I going to face him?* The quiet click of the bathroom door echoed out in the otherwise silent living room. Lost in thought, Mark hadn't noticed the sound of the shower come to a stop. *I guess I'm going to find out*, he thought bleakly.

Cliff quietly stepped to the bedroom to check on his guest. Finding Mark alert, he entered the room and said, "Oh, you're awake. Hope I didn't wake you." He then asked cheerfully, "How's the patient?"

"No, you didn't wake me. I don't usually sleep this late," Mark replied. "My arm aches a little. Everything seems to be sore, but I'll live. I was just thinking I should be going."

Cliff was wearing gym pants and had a towel draped over his bare shoulders. "Going? Where?" he asked, surprised. Keeping his eyes on Mark, he tossed the towel absentmindedly to a laundry basket tucked into the corner of the room by the dresser.

"Oh, well... home, I guess. I thought you would be happy to get rid of me. I didn't want...," Mark stumbled over the familiar phrase and then finished it with a shy smile, "to be a bother." He wondered at Cliff's surprise. Surely, the big guy didn't want him to hang around.

In the shower, Cliff had sided with that part of his mind that wanted things to go back the way they had been, all neat and tidy. He would take Mark home, and that would be that. Faced with the reality of letting the little guy go, he faltered. The voice that advised him to get it over with and let him go was losing. Cliff didn't want to listen. Instead, he said evenly, "I figured that since I would be taking you back to your appointment at the clinic later, well, I figured we could spend the time together 'til then."

Mark had completely forgotten the appointment. "You don't have to."

"I would like to," Cliff admitted, much to his own surprise.

Mark was at a loss, but if Cliff didn't want him to go, he wasn't going to disagree. "Okay," he replied, though a little doubtfully.

"Did you want to take a shower?" Cliff asked. He felt more relaxed now that the immediate threat of Mark leaving had passed.

"Yeah, that would be great. I really need to brush my teeth, though. Do you think we could go by my place before this evening?" Mark did his best to make himself at least appear at ease.

"Sure, I can take you there after you shower. I'm going to have breakfast first. Do you eat breakfast?" Cliff enquired of Mark, his mood uncharacteristically cheerful.

"I usually just have cereal or toast," Mark answered.

"Same here. I'll get something ready while you get cleaned up." Cliff turned and walked out of the room.

Mark picked up his underwear and the shorts from the floor beside the bed. He managed after a little struggle to get the shorts on. There was no way he was going to walk across the apartment naked.

In the bathroom, he cautiously pulled the sling off and adjusted the water in the shower. Other than bumping his elbow twice against the wall in the unfamiliar space, he got through it well enough. Drying off after the shower was more of a challenge, but Mark did the best he could. Presentable again, sling on, and only disappointed at not having the chance to brush his teeth, Mark walked back into the living room.

The job of showering with his injured arm in the way had occupied Mark's attention so fully that he hadn't even thought about the situation he was in. *Just as well*, he decided, once he had to face it again.

Cliff didn't have a kitchen table in his apartment. The kitchen was far too small for one to fit, so Cliff usually took his meals on the couch. Besides, it wasn't like he did a lot of entertaining. While Mark was busy in the bathroom, Cliff waited in the living room with a simple breakfast for two arranged on the coffee table in front of him. He could hear the occasional bumps, grunts, and exclamations coming from the bathroom. He resisted the urge to go and offer to help. It impressed him how resilient the little guy was. Stubborn certainly, but resilient.

Mark was wearing the borrowed shorts again. There was no chance of his putting on his T-shirt without assistance. He felt a little embarrassed to be shirtless. Cliff didn't seem to notice his discomfort, though. Breakfast was waiting and so was Cliff, Mark noted. As Mark sat down, a realization struck him. *How does one eat cereal on a couch with one hand?*

"There's no bread for toast," Cliff said in apology. "I was running to get some last night when I bumped into you." The memory brought on a pang of guilt.

Mark slipped off the couch and dropped down to the floor as gracefully as he could. Once settled, he pulled one of the bowls closer. At least this way he wouldn't make a complete mess while he ate.

"I never thought of that. Sorry," Cliff said, comprehending what Mark was doing. He moved to the other side of the coffee table and sat on the floor as well, though with much less elegance to the maneuver than Mark had displayed.

Mark couldn't help the little laugh as he watched the bigger man sit down heavily.

"Hey! I'm being polite," Cliff said, mock-angry.

"Right," Mark replied, straight-faced.

Cliff threw a nugget of dry cereal that hit Mark squarely in the chest.

THE LAST SNOW OF WINTER

"Ouch!" Mark exaggerated. "Oh, do you know where my backpack is?" He asked the question as he searched for the errant bit of cereal.

"It's still in the car," Cliff said as he poured the milk for both of them.

"Good, I was afraid I lost it." Mark picked up a spoon.

"Do you have schoolwork to do today?" Cliff had hoped they could spend the time together and was a little disappointed. Then he felt foolish for feeling that way.

"I had planned to, but...." Mark shrugged and looked to his injured arm. "I can write some with my left hand. Not well, though."

Cliff suddenly felt very guilty. "I'm sorry for all this."

"Hey, it was an accident, and not the first one for me, I might add. Trust me; I come from a long line of clumsy. I'll manage somehow." Mark wasn't as convinced as he tried to sound, but there was no point worrying about it. He would deal with it as it came.

They ate quietly. When they finished, Mark shuffled back from the coffee table and rose in a smooth, easy motion. Cliff was impressed. He had to struggle to get up from the same position, supporting himself with a hand on the table. Mark chuckled. Cliff looked to the other man.

"The advantage of being svelte," Mark said, smiling, sweeping one hand down his side as he arched his body sinuously.

"You shit. It's not a fair contest." Cliff appraised Mark's body. *Yes, svelte suited. Long and lean like a cat.* "Come on, Bobcat. If you're going to give me grief, you can help clean up."

They carried the dishes and things into the kitchen. The room was too small for the two of them, so Mark went back and picked up the last few items from the coffee table as Cliff rinsed out the bowls.

"Do you need help getting dressed?" Cliff asked as Mark returned with the milk.

"What?" The question surprised Mark. Then he remembered his arm. "Oh, um, probably... yes." *No point being proud*, he reasoned.

"Let's go." Cliff gestured toward the bedroom.

I wish, Mark thought, wanting something else entirely. He picked up his shirt and retrieved his jeans from the chair by the door. Then he walked to the bedroom where the other man was waiting. Cliff took the shirt and jeans from Mark, placed them on the bed, and indicated that the other man should drop the gym shorts.

Cliff knelt down, holding the jeans for Mark to step into them. It had seemed like it would be a simple procedure. In reality, the two men struggled to get the jeans on without knocking Mark over. The comedy of the situation helped to distract Mark from the combination of excitement and embarrassment he was experiencing. More than once, he had to reach out and grab the broad shoulder of the other man to keep from falling. Finally, Cliff buttoned the fly of Mark's jeans. Mark held his breath without noticing he was doing so.

Putting on the T-shirt was even more of an ordeal than the jeans and much less amusing. However, Cliff was surprisingly gentle, and they managed the task together. Eventually, Mark was dressed and his injured arm safely positioned in the sling. Cliff brushed his hands over Mark's shoulders to smooth the fabric of his shirt. Involuntarily, Mark shivered in reaction to the touch and closed his eyes.

"Are you okay? Did I hurt you?" Cliff's voice was quiet and intimate. He was still holding Mark by the shoulders.

"No, I'm fine." Mark took a breath, looked at Cliff, and assumed a smile. "Thanks. I'll wait out there and let you change in private." Mark grabbed his socks from the floor and left the room.

Cliff watched him go.

Mark sat on the couch. He knew he was developing a serious crush on Cliff. He hadn't let himself do something like that since high school. That had been a disaster. *Nothing good is going to come of this crush either*, he warned himself. He attempted to pull his socks on one-handed but hadn't gotten very far when Cliff entered the room.

"Why won't you let me help you?" Cliff asked, annoyed.

Resigned, Mark sighed, held out the socks, and said, "Can you help me, please?"

Cliff took the socks, knelt down, and slipped them on Mark's feet just a little roughly.

"Thank you." Mark continued, "I find it hard to ask for help. I try to be so self-sufficient, so... perfect."

"Why?" The confession surprised Cliff. He wanted to understand.

"To prove my worth, I guess," Mark said.

"What? Prove it to whom?" Cliff asked in confusion.

"Oh, to my family, to society, and to myself, I guess." Mark looked at Cliff. "I know better. I'm not a fool." He turned away, feeling foolish despite his words.

Cliff sat beside him. His annoyance faded. He could understand what Mark was saying. Placing his arm across Mark's back, he leaned in and said, "I'd like to be your friend. You don't need to prove anything to me."

Not trusting himself to speak, Mark could only nod his head to indicate that he had heard.

"You ready to go?" Cliff asked gently.

Mark nodded his head again.

They walked to the door.

"Would you tie my laces?" Mark asked.

"Yes, I will." Cliff replied in a playful tone, "Now, was that so hard?"

"No," Mark grumbled, rolling his eyes.

Cliff knelt to help Mark, slapping the smaller man's thigh in a show of good humor. He stood, and they both finished dressing. Cliff only assisted Mark when he saw it was necessary. He didn't want to push the little guy too much.

Chapter 7

Snow had fallen through the night. A woolly blanket of white carpeted the ground and delicately traced even the smallest branches of the trees perfectly. Everything looked clean and new, glistening in the sunlight. Mark's face was bright in admiration of the sight. Cliff stared, taken in by the radiance of the other man. He forced himself to look away and observe their surroundings instead. It was a beautiful morning. He hadn't noticed before.

At the foot of the stairs, the two men engaged in a slight disagreement about whether or not to take the car. Mark was all for walking. Cliff worried that it was too far for Mark to hike right now.

"I walk it at least twice a day," Mark insisted impatiently. "Come on. It's beautiful out. Or can't you walk that far?" Mark teased.

Cliff's little friend amused him. *Yup, he's a bobcat for sure.* He gave in willingly but insisted he would carry Mark's backpack. Mark seemed about to argue but huffed and handed the bag over.

They walked silently at first. Mark had to remind himself periodically to slow down. When alone (and he was usually alone), he tended to walk fast. He continued to admire the scenery. Cliff watched Mark covertly, caught in the novelty of experiencing the beauty around him through the other man's eyes. As the tension left over from their conversation on the couch passed, they began chatting comfortably.

"So how come I've never seen you around before this year?" Cliff asked conversationally. "I know you can't be in your first year."

"I'm in my fourth year," Mark confirmed. "But I've spent most of my time at the other end of campus in the science buildings." A line of sight opened to the left. This one house, unlike its neighbors, sat well away from the road to command a view of the dike land beyond. A generous lawn filled the space between. It was Mark's favorite house in town. "How about you, what are you studying?"

Cliff followed Mark's gaze. A clean field of white sparkled and danced with sunlight. "I'm working on a BA in Psychology," Cliff said without emphasis. "I'm in my fifth year. It's hard to fit in a full course load with football," he explained quickly. He didn't want Mark to think he was slow. "So you're not in Arts?" he asked, his eyes on the landscape but his mind on the man walking beside him. Cliff was mildly surprised. He had assumed Mark was taking an arts degree. He shook his head in an effort to cast off his own prejudices.

Distracted by the view, Mark hadn't noticed Cliff's surprise."No, no, science. I'm taking pre-vet," he replied.

"Then what's with the painting clothes?" Cliff had observed that Mark often came to one of the classes they shared wearing a loose white shirt blotched with numerous colorful paint stains.

"Oh that. I take painting just after philosophy. There's no time to go home, and it's easier to change beforehand." Now that Mark considered it, he was a little embarrassed. "I suppose it looks sloppy." He hadn't been concerned with trying to impress anyone. He was amazed that Cliff had noticed at all.

"No worse than what anybody else wears," Cliff remarked honestly. He often dressed in gym clothes for class. "So you're going to be a vet, huh?"

"If I get accepted on the island," Mark answered casually. Looking to the other man, he realized Cliff hadn't caught the reference. He then added, "UPEI." The nearest vet college was part of the university on the tiny island province. The veterinary school only took twenty new students each year. Mark had applied already. His grades so far were good enough, but the final decision depended on exams and, of course, the other applicants. It would be summer before he would know for sure, but Mark was confident in his chances. He had worked very hard to get this far.

"Is that what you love?" Cliff asked. He wanted to know more about what made the other man tick.

The question threw him. Mark had to stop and think. He stopped walking without being aware of it. Cliff, who had walked on a few steps, turned back to face him. Mark replied, speaking slowly, "I don't know. I don't know what I love." Neither man spoke for a moment. Then Mark came to himself, began walking again, and asked, "What about you, what do you love?"

"Football," Cliff affirmed automatically. He fell into step with the other man to walk side by side again. "I've always wanted to play pro, as long as I can remember." It was a dream that seemed to go back to his childhood. "You don't feel the same way about being a vet?"

"No, I think I'd be a good vet, but it isn't something I've always wanted to do." Mark was suddenly uneasy about that.

"Then why do it?" Cliff's desire to play pro football was so ingrained he couldn't imagine someone not having a similar dream to follow.

"I think I would enjoy being a vet. I like working with animals." That was true. "Besides, it would be a socially acceptable career for an overly creative single male, at least in the eyes of my extended family and their neighbors." Mark presented the declaration in a running singsong tone. Resigned to his future, he was sure his parents and family would be proud of him as a vet, especially if he remained a confirmed bachelor for the rest of his life. *Throw a wife and children into the mix, and they would be completely satisfied, but they can't have everything*, he mused darkly.

Cliff was finding it hard to understand his new friend. *How could someone who appears so fiercely independent bury his own desires like that?* It didn't make sense to him.

"I can tell you disagree," Mark said, looking sideways to catch his companion's expression. "I'm not blind to the mistakes I make. It's hard growing up believing people will despise you if they discover what you really are." After a pause, he continued, "I've known I was gay a long time. I knew it before I knew it. To compensate for being…

THE LAST SNOW OF WINTER

evil, whatever," Mark said, cringing and shivering in disgust at the word, "I needed to be the best. Never ask for help. Be perfect." Mark stopped talking and turned his head away sharply.

Cliff realized he could understand after all. Wasn't he doing something similar, sacrificing part of himself for an illusion? Was it dedication or was it fear that stopped him from doing what he really wanted to do, taking what he really wanted to take? He didn't have an answer. He finally said, "I can't judge you. I'm no better than you. I'm sorry."

Mark wasn't sure what Cliff meant by this declaration. He let it go for now, saying instead, "I've worked through and cleared away a lot of the crap left over from my childhood. I wasn't kidding about low self-esteem. Just when I think I have it all figured out, I walk headlong into a trap." Mark paused and considered their earlier conversation. Cliff had offered to be his friend. That was a valuable thing. Deciding, Mark said, "I would like to have you as a friend."

Cliff remembered. He could feel his attachment for Mark growing. He felt out of control again, and for the first time in his life, he didn't care. They didn't say much more 'til they arrived at a row of neat little cottages set back from the main road. Mark led the way to one of them. He struggled to retrieve his keys from his right coat pocket. Cliff felt the urge to help but refrained, deciding to choose his battles instead. Eventually Mark had the door open, and they stepped inside.

"Home," Mark announced with a sweeping wave of his good arm, inviting Cliff in. "Make yourself at home. I'm going to brush my teeth and change…." Mark paused. Cliff looked at him with one brow raised and battle ready. "If you will help me," Mark finished, sounding resigned.

Cliff nodded and watched as Mark disappeared into the bathroom. Maybe they were making progress. Now alone, he looked around the living room. Near an open door that Cliff saw led to a dark, cave-like bedroom, an unusual painting hung on the wall. It captured his attention. The artwork didn't suit the rest of the traditional motel-like decor. Perhaps this was Mark's doing. On closer inspection, Cliff noticed the small signature in the corner of the painting. Sure enough, it was Mark's own work. He stepped back to take it in just as Mark reentered the room.

"Oh, what do you think?" Mark asked on seeing Cliff examining his work. He was curious what the big guy might say.

What do I think? The subject of the painting was what appeared to be a shepherd, but the shepherd had the head of a lion. It was wet in the scene, maybe even raining. The shepherd was wearing a long, heavy oilskin against the weather. He was walking out of the brush cradling a lamb gently with a dog trailing behind. The image felt familiar, beautiful, and yet slightly disturbing. Cliff shook his head. He worried he didn't know enough about art to give an intelligent answer.

When the other man didn't say anything, Mark added, "You won't hurt my feelings if you don't like it."

"Oh, I do like it!" Cliff replied quickly and honestly. "I just don't think I understand what it means." He then added, "I guess I didn't want to say something that would make me sound like an ignorant jock."

Mark chuckled faintly. He was slightly surprised that Cliff would care what Mark thought of him. He stated sincerely, "I already know better."

Cliff looked back to the painting feeling faintly warmed by Mark's words. He considered the image and said, "It feels… religious to me, somehow."

"It feels that way to me too." Mark looked from Cliff to the painting. It was one of his favorite works. "But it's different for everyone. I just paint it. I can't control what people see there."

"I had no idea you were this talented," Cliff remarked. His little bobcat was full of surprises. Cliff was then mildly shocked to discover that he was beginning to think of this man as his.

Mark replied noncommittally, "I have talent, but I have a lot to learn. I'm not that good."

Cliff found that hard to believe but let the comment pass unchallenged.

After a moment of quiet, Mark asked, "Would you help me change?"

"Yup, lead the way." Cliff looked back one last time to the image of the shepherd on the wall.

Mark turned and walked to a door Cliff hadn't noticed earlier and entered another room. Cliff followed. He noted pleasantly that the bedroom smelled like Mark, though he was at a loss to describe it. The room was bright with sunlight. "You and your roommate are not... together?" Cliff asked. He didn't want to ask but felt the need to know.

"No! No, Jeff's straight. We're just friends." The question surprised Mark, but he figured it was fair for the other man to ask.

"Does he know... about you?" Cliff felt awkward. He then admonished himself for feeling that such a simple question was too personal. *Hell, you slept in the same bed. He's seen you naked!*

"I think so, yes. We don't talk about it, but yeah, he knows." Mark and Jeff had been friends since first year and roommates for the last two. Nothing romantic, they were just good friends. Mark began rummaging through his things, looking for something that would be easy to manage. He really needed to do a wash. Eventually he found a pair of faded camouflage pants he had picked up from a surplus store. He usually only wore them around the house, especially when he had to do laundry. They were button fly again, but at least they were clean and easy to put on. He then pulled out a short-sleeve button-up shirt and considered it. It would do. He undid his jeans and stepped out of them, picking them up and tossing them into the full basket in the closet. Realization dawned. "I'll need to change my underwear," he said, face red with embarrassment.

"Go ahead. I saw it all yesterday, remember?" Cliff teased.

"It was dark then," Mark protested.

"Fine." Cliff turned around with an exaggerated huff. "You'll never make it in the locker room."

It was clear Cliff wasn't going to make this any easier. Mark pulled off his underwear awkwardly and changed into a clean pair as quickly as he could. "I have no plans of ever being in a locker room." While he wasn't completely hopeless at sports, Mark hadn't enjoyed gym in school. The rampant teenage homophobia of his classmates combined with his budding sexuality made for an unpleasant combination. As soon as it was no longer required, Mark gave up gym class happily. "I'm not used to having strangers see me naked."

"What about when you date?" After asking the question, Cliff was uncomfortable. Was that too far? It wasn't any of his business, after all.

"I don't date," Mark answered flatly.

"Really, not at all? What, a good-looking guy like yourself? Why not?" *This is dangerous territory.* Cliff was certain he was going too far with the questions but was genuinely interested and couldn't resist.

"You're sweet," Mark replied self-consciously. "I don't date because I'm chicken. I'm afraid to walk up to a strange guy and ask if he would like to go out. Most of them are straight, you know. On the few occasions when someone showed an interest in me, I was so oblivious that I missed the chance. I did ask out one guy last year...."

When Mark didn't finish, Cliff asked, "What happened?"

"He was straight." Mark flushed remembering the incident. "He took it well. I was embarrassed as hell."

Cliff couldn't help but laugh. "Are you done with your underwear already?" he asked in good humor.

"Decent!" Mark affirmed, looking down at himself.

Cliff turned to face Mark again. "Pants first?" Another comedy of errors played out, but the two men managed to get Mark dressed again. "What about going to a gay bar?" Cliff asked when they had finished. "In the city?" Cliff couldn't understand why he kept asking these questions. "You could meet someone there." *It's like watching a train wreck*, he thought. *It keeps on going and going in a long, slow chain reaction with no hope of stopping it.*

For a few seconds before responding, Mark considered the idea of visiting a bar to pick up a date. "That isn't what I want. Sex is great, but what I want is companionship." He paused and then added, "I know it sounds silly. What I want is to have someone to fall asleep with and wake up with and do the dishes with, all the boring stuff." Though Mark knew it sounded silly, it was what he wanted. David had laughed at first when Mark told him the same.

"I don't think that's silly." Changing the subject because he didn't know what else to say, Cliff asked, "What would you like to do today? What were you going to do today?"

"I had planned to do laundry," Mark said, looking at the overflowing basket in the closet, "But it can wait. I could go to the computer lab and work on a paper." He wondered at the other man's apparent interest in spending time with him. "What about you?"

"I have some reading to do. And I have a sick friend I was going to spend time with." When Mark didn't react, Cliff smiled broadly. "I mean you, stupid."

"I'm not sick." Mark couldn't help the happy feeling that filled him. "But thanks, I'd like that."

After a brief discussion, they decided that Mark should work on his paper in the computer lab. First, they would walk back to Cliff's place and have lunch. Then Cliff could grab a few books and accompany Mark to the library. While he preferred reading at home, he could manage well enough in the library this one time. They walked back to town talking and getting to know each other better. They vigilantly avoided certain topics. Even during a lunch of cold pizza, they kept the conversation light and safe. Both men seemed to feel the need to pull back a bit, perhaps anxious at how open they had been so far.

Chapter 8

Completed just the year before, the computer lab was one part of a new addition to the campus. A two-story glass and steel structure now filled the gap between the library and the B.A.C. The addition provided space for a new combined entrance to the buildings, an area for microfiche storage, and the computer lab. The lab housed a collection of state-of-the-art Macintosh computers. Students required permission from their head of department to have the privilege of using the expensive machines. Mark was lucky. The professor who instructed Population Ecology was a computer nut and insisted his students use the machines to run population simulations. Mark was pleased to have a pass. Most students wrote out their papers longhand and took them to the copy center to have them typed up. Mark preferred to do his own typing but wasn't very good at it. The word processor turned out to be an unforeseen godsend.

Promising to come back in a few hours, Cliff left Mark at the door to the computer lab. Two other students were busy clattering away at their respective workstations as Mark took a seat. Within minutes, they each packed up and left separately. Except for Mark, the lab was now empty. It was unusual for the room to be so quiet. Most days a person was lucky to find a free station.

More than an hour had passed before Mark leaned back from the keyboard and stretched as best he could. Progress was slow since he could only use his left hand, but he was making headway. Unfortunately, he was also beginning to feel worn-out. The unfamiliar action of typing with just his off hand was straining his neck. His right arm ached too. The Tylenol he had taken before coming didn't seem to

THE LAST SNOW OF WINTER

be making any difference. Mark considered going to look for Cliff. No, he decided, they both had things to do. He didn't want to bother him. Instead, he pushed on stubbornly.

In the lounge on the second floor of the library, Cliff slouched in one of the low retro-styled chairs that were scattered about the area in little groupings. A row of floor to ceiling windows gave him a partial view of the treed park in front of University Hall. He looked out over the bare trees, not really seeing them, wondering instead how Mark was faring. Cliff had caught himself rereading the same lines several times. He knew he was too distracted to study properly. He needed to clear his head and focus.

Deciding to take a walk, Cliff closed his book, collected his things, and stuffed them into a bag. Maybe he could find a better place to read. He really preferred reading at home. He was more comfortable there. He didn't like people watching him. Not that there were many people around today. The place was practically dead. However, Cliff usually felt eyes following him. *Yes, the jock can read*, he thought angrily in response to imagined looks of disbelief. Mark had been right, he realized uneasily. Cliff did like that he intimidated most people. It made him feel lonely, but it was safer. The idea shocked him. Spending time with Mark had started him thinking about things he didn't necessarily want to think about. He was a different person with Mark. He couldn't get the man out of his head. Cliff wandered aimlessly away from the lounge, lost in thought.

Fifteen minutes later, only mildly surprised, Cliff found himself standing opposite the glass partition wall that flanked the entrance to the computer lab. He could see Mark working away diligently, alone in the muted light, face lit by the tiny glowing screen. It was obvious he was struggling. While he watched, Mark tried to loosen up his shoulders and then rubbed the back of his neck absently with one hand. Cliff pushed open the door. The hum of the ventilation system and the carpeting on the floor rendered his approach silent.

Mark started when he felt a touch on his shoulder. Turning to discover Cliff standing behind him, he exclaimed with a laugh, "You nearly gave me a heart attack!" Mark relaxed and stretched his neck to work out a kink.

Cliff didn't take his hand away. Instead, he moved closer and began massaging Mark's shoulders. A storm was raging inside, but Cliff didn't let it show. Mark was clearly enjoying the touch of his hands. The physical connection felt good for him too. Cliff didn't entirely trust his voice but felt the need to say something. His already deep voice was slightly husky as he asked, "How is the paper going?" He continued massaging the other man's neck and shoulders as he waited for a reply.

The combination of the touch and tone sent a shiver up Mark's spine. He didn't want to wake from this dream. If only Cliff wanted the same thing. *He knows you're gay*, his mind whispered yet again. Another voice countered: *He would have said something if he was interested.*

Enough! Mark closed his eyes and didn't respond.

"I thought I would make supper tonight," Cliff said. "We could eat early and then go to your appointment." His voice sounded more like its normal self.

"Aren't you tired of me yet?" Mark asked, afraid of the answer. Tipping his head back, he looked up at the man still standing behind him.

"No," Cliff responded. "Are you tired of me?"

Surprised, Mark answered honestly, "No."

"Good." Cliff didn't know how this would work out, but he knew he wanted to keep Mark around. "I'll have to pick up a few things at the store. Do you need more time?"

Mark leaned forward to grab the mouse. He saved his work and logged off the computer. "I'm ready. I was too sore to work much longer anyway."

Cliff carried both of their bags as they set off.

Chapter 9

THE grocery store was on their way. Mark felt a little out of place trailing behind his burly friend, who was pushing the cart. He watched as Cliff picked up a loaf of French bread, ground meat, and a jar of pasta sauce.

"I'm not much of a cook," Cliff apologized, "but I promise not to poison you."

At the checkout, Mark offered to pay, but the other man refused. They argued some, but Cliff got his way. It was then that a voice rang out over the heads of the startled shoppers and cashiers.

"Yo! Clifford!"

Jumping slightly, Mark looked up to find the source of the disturbance. The owner of the bull-like voice was standing just inside the main doors about ten meters away. The guy wasn't quite as big as Cliff but looked like he could easily be a teammate. Mark watched him raise an arm in a sort of salute toward Cliff. He then walked away apparently on his own errand. Mark was amused. Clifford? It reminded him of the storybook character.

Surprised by the call, Cliff recovered quickly. He indifferently raised a hand in acknowledgement, relieved to see Jack moving away. For a moment, he was terrified that Jack would come over. Jack had such a big mouth and no class. He would have asked who Mark was. Cliff then despised himself for being such a chickenshit. He would not be ashamed of Mark. He collected the bags and moved for the door.

They were walking toward the duck pond. Not a word had passed between them since leaving the grocery store. The incident at the checkout hadn't made much of an impression on Mark, so he was comfortable in the silence. *Clifford?* The name had stuck. Mark toyed with the name in his head.

Cliff hadn't said anything since seeing Jack. The silence didn't sit as comfortably with him as it did Mark. His reaction to Jack's presence had thrown him. *Why should I care what Jack thinks? I'm not doing anything wrong.*

"So... Clifford?" Mark asked playfully. He was unable to refrain from trying out the name any longer.

"No." Cliff responded in a tone that made his feelings about the name quite clear.

"Whatever you say, Cliffor—"

"Don't even think it." Cliff's humor was returning. "You're lucky my hands are full," he threatened.

"Ah-ah, no roughhousing," Mark reminded. "I'm still in a weakened state." Mark quickly moved ahead, turned, and then walked backward a few meters away.

"Weak my ass, I don't believe a word of it." Cliff made as if to run at the other man. He shook off his thoughts of Jack. *Who cares what other people might think?* He wouldn't let this be taken from him, even if it was only a fantasy.

Mark increased the distance between them, just in case. He didn't think Cliff would do anything too terrible, but why take chances? He turned back to see Cliff still walking sedately some distance away, book bags in one hand and a grocery bag in the other.

"Get back here, Bobcat," Cliff said with a smile.

That smile disarmed Mark. He had never suspected Cliff could look that way. His usually icy blue eyes were soft and sparkled in harmony with the expression. If Cliff had asked him right then, Mark would have done anything he wanted. He stood still and waited for Cliff to catch up. Falling in beside him as he walked, Mark asked, "Bobcat?"

"It fits, I think," Cliff replied.

"How so?" Mark wanted to know. He had never had a nickname before.

"Another time, Bobcat. We need to get supper ready." Cliff lifted the grocery bag and shook it as if to make his point.

Mark was astonished at the transformation in Cliff's behavior. He suddenly seemed completely comfortable, almost loveable. Mark didn't know what had changed but was prepared to enjoy it while it lasted.

Cliff's playful attitude grew exponentially once they entered the apartment. He helped Mark out of his winter clothes, touching him casually perhaps more than was necessary. They began making supper together, but between the cramped quarters of the kitchen and the fact that Mark could do little to help with one free hand, Cliff eventually banished the smaller man to the couch. Cliff put on some music and sang along as he prepared the meal. He felt free and happy.

Listening bemusedly as the man butchered perfectly good songs with an admittedly sexy bass voice, Mark wondered again at the change. He got up and walked back to the kitchen to get a better view of this strange performance.

Cliff nearly walked into Mark when he stepped out of the kitchen with a glass in each hand. They stood chest to chest for a suspended moment of time before Mark backed up to give the other man room. In response, Cliff stepped forward, closing the space between them again. Then he leaned in and kissed Mark decisively. The kiss was passionate and slightly rough. Cliff felt rather than heard Mark make a quiet noise of pleasure. He growled softly in reply and fell deeper into the kiss.

Mark registered Cliff's growl. He felt the other man's tongue touch his lip. He had never experienced anything like this. How long it lasted, he couldn't say. Finally, Cliff backed away and placed the glasses he was still holding on the counter. He turned back and took Mark in his arms, kissing him again forcefully. They broke apart when Mark grunted in discomfort, his injured arm caught between them.

"I wanted to do that so much," Cliff growled, referring to the kiss. His voice was deep and husky. He stole another quick kiss and then motioned Mark to the couch.

Not knowing what would happen next, Mark watched as Cliff returned to the kitchen. The familiar sounds of food preparation filtered into the living room. Within a minute, Cliff walked out with the two glasses again.

"I wish I had wine for us," Cliff said as he sat down. "It would be more romantic." He leaned in to kiss Mark lightly one more time. "That feels so good."

"I think I missed a step," Mark said. The attention thrilled him, but it felt a little surreal.

"I'm sorry." Cliff was almost too happy to contain himself, but he owed Mark an explanation. "I guess I've always been an all or none kind of guy." Collecting himself, he stated, "I like you."

"I gathered!" Mark's blurted response was humorously sarcastic. He was pleased at what he was hearing but still felt a little bewildered.

An angry buzzing sound from the kitchen drew their attention. Cliff got up and made a wait sign to the other man. In less than five minutes, he returned with steaming plates of spaghetti, making a second trip for the garlic bread.

Mark dropped onto the floor again to be closer to his plate. Cliff was tempted to sit beside him but opted to sit opposite instead. "I want to explain," he said.

Mark looked to the other man expectantly.

"It's hard for me," Cliff admitted. "I'll need a little time. So I can make it make sense."

Mark ate a little and considered what had happened. "Are you playing with me?" he asked seriously.

Surprised, Cliff replied, "No. No! That's not it at all." He hadn't thought this through. He sighed and rubbed his forehead. "I've done this all wrong." He tried desperately to arrange his thoughts. He needed

THE LAST SNOW OF WINTER

Mark to understand. "I like you. It's just… football players can't be gay."

"I don't… what?" Mark heard the words but didn't seem to be getting the meaning.

Cliff clarified, "Professional football players can't be gay. They can't be out."

Light was beginning to dawn for Mark, but he still had a long way to go before he would feel comfortable in his understanding. He asked, "Okay. What suddenly changed this evening?"

"I don't know." Cliff considered. "I guess I was tired of being miserable." The change had come on gradually but had broken so suddenly it was still hard for him to understand. Back on the street, walking from the grocery store, Cliff had suddenly felt weightless, as if experiencing freedom for the first time. *You can thank Jack for that.* No, Cliff had to be honest. Jack might have been the trigger, but the truth was that shame was at the root of his transformation. Cliff had felt ashamed. Not ashamed of Mark; he refused to feel that way. He loved his little bobcat. *Loved? Easy, big guy*, a voice cautioned, *you're just overexcited.* No, he wasn't ashamed of Mark, so why should he be ashamed to be with Mark? *Why should I be ashamed of myself?* The feeling of shame had made him angry. It was then that Cliff had finally let it all go.

Cliff wanted to explain everything to Mark, but he just couldn't seem to find the words. Stalling, he promised instead, "I'll tell you everything later. We still have to get to your appointment." Cliff hoped Mark would be patient.

Appointment? Mark had forgotten his appointment with the doctor at six. He looked for his watch, remembering too late that it was on his bedside table at home. Unsettled, he turned his attention back to his plate.

They rushed through eating, saying little. Mark felt adrift. After helping him on with his boots and coat, Cliff kissed him again, cradling Mark's face gently in strong hands. Mark let himself enjoy the touch. The kisses were addictive. He could sense the strength and power in the man. It was intoxicating. However, unsure of his footing, Mark held himself back. The change was too fast. The unknowns frightened him.

Sensing Mark's reserve, Cliff burned with the need to make him understand. He was afraid he was messing it all up. They got into the car and started for the medical center. Was it really just a day ago that Cliff had found himself practically lying on top of this guy on a street corner? It seemed impossible. The time between had transformed him. He shook his head and put his attention into driving.

Chapter 10

THE clinic wasn't empty this evening. A half-dozen other people were scattered around the waiting room. Some were alone and some in pairs. Mark announced himself to the receptionist. It was the same woman from the night before. She asked him to take a seat, telling him it shouldn't be too long a wait. Less than ten minutes passed before a voice called Mark's name. Not sure if he was welcome, Cliff hung back. Mark was already in the exam room before he noticed he was alone.

Dr. Park asked a few questions as she examined Mark's elbow and head. "Everything looks good," she observed. "The swelling has gone down." She nodded as if agreeing with herself. "No surgery unless something changes. I will refer you for physio. Check with reception for the schedule. We will want to start right away. Keep the sling on for now." Changing the subject, she asked, "How is your friend?"

Mark, unprepared for the question, took a moment to reply. "Umm, he's fine. He's out in the waiting room."

"Good," said the doctor in response. She looked at Mark thoughtfully and said, "He cares for you." Seeing the questioning look on Mark's face, she explained, "He has been in and out of this clinic often enough over the last few years. I can't say I know him all that well, though. I was afraid he didn't let anyone really get to know him." Her eyes took on a faraway look for a moment before she added, "He's a good guy. It's nice to see he has a friend." She abruptly became more businesslike again, directed Mark toward the exit, excused herself, and headed off to her next patient.

Mark returned to the waiting area considering the unusual exchange. It was just one more confusing event to add to the collection. He found Cliff fidgeting nervously in a too-small chair. Mark smiled inwardly at the sight. Stepping toward the big man, he remembered the physiotherapy appointment. Mark turned back to the receptionist. He felt rather than saw Cliff come up and stand close behind him.

Cliff had been waiting uncomfortably since Mark had left him. He shifted repeatedly in his chair, thinking absently that he would like to meet the person who'd designed them. The chair wasn't the real problem, though. What was really eating at him was the memory of how he had bungled the situation with Mark. In his excitement, he had let himself be carried away and had carelessly swept Mark off with him. It was a relief when he looked up to see Mark finally reenter the waiting room. As Cliff watched, his new friend made two steps toward him with a strange look on his face. Then he stopped and turned back to the reception desk. Cliff was determined to fix this. He had to. He walked up to where Mark was still talking with the receptionist. Once she handed over an appointment card, Cliff asked, "How did it go? Is everything okay?"

Mark turned to face the big man. He could feel his concern. Maybe that was what suddenly gave Mark butterflies. "So far so good," he answered with a composure he didn't feel. "The doctor wants me to start physio right away." Trying to lessen the other man's anxiety, Mark added, "See, nothing to worry about. No permanent harm done." Mark was surprised when Cliff reached out and grasped his good arm firmly and pulled him closer. It was a decidedly familiar gesture, Mark thought, for such a public place.

Remembering himself, Cliff let go of Mark's arm and stepped back. "Are you ready to go?" he asked.

"Sure."

"Can we go somewhere to talk?" Cliff's heart was beating fast as he asked the question. It was time to 'fess up, but he was afraid Mark wouldn't give him a chance to explain.

"Yes, of course." Mark wondered at Cliff's earnestness. He fell into step behind him as Cliff turned and led the way to the car.

Cliff drove the car to Wolfville's tiny wharf. It was located not far from the train station. Mark knew the spot well. To the left and right, remnants of earthen dikes built by the Acadians trailed off into the visible distance. The dikes separated low-lying fields from the tides of the Minas Basin. Like many others, Mark enjoyed walking atop the dikes. At least he did when the weather was a little warmer.

In the glare from the headlights, Mark couldn't tell if the tide was in or out tonight. There could be water just past the low wall surrounding the wharf or a ten-foot drop onto red mud. Just a few weeks ago, the last time Mark was there, massive slabs of ice had littered the exposed mudflats. The miniature icebergs, left behind by the retreating tide, had dotted the landscape as far as the eye could see. Mark suddenly wished he could see the water. It wasn't like being next to the ocean, but it reminded him of it. Walking the shore by the ocean always seemed to calm him. Not sure what to expect, Mark waited patiently to see what Cliff would do next.

Cliff parked the car facing the wharf. He turned off the headlights and then cut the engine. Silence enveloped them. Behind the car, the lights of town burned brightly. Through the windshield spread a vast, dark expanse relieved only occasionally by clusters of lights indicating distant homes and communities. The glow from behind saved the car's interior from being in total darkness, but it left their faces in shadow. Cliff didn't mind. He didn't think he could have this conversation sitting face to face in his well-lit apartment.

"Are you warm enough?" Cliff asked, avoiding the conversation a little longer. He noted distantly that Mark had nodded in response to the question. Time to make good, he realized. "First, I want to apologize for making you uncomfortable earlier," Cliff began. "I guess I got a little carried away." At the time, he had been so overjoyed that he forgot that Mark wasn't really his, as much as he had been thinking it was so. He waited a moment to see if Mark would respond. When he didn't, Cliff went on. "I also need to confess that I've been thinking about you for a few months now."

"What?" The admission truly astonished Mark.

"I'm not out," Cliff admitted. "But I know I'm... gay." He swallowed. This was harder than he had even imagined it would be. "I keep it quiet. You know why."

Mark remembered the statement about pro football players not being gay. "I understand." Even he, as a non-fan, knew the world of pro sports could still be highly homophobic.

Nodding, Cliff continued. "I went out with girls in high school to keep up appearances." The memory humiliated Cliff. The girls had been friends. He let them and everyone else believe there was more to it. There was no excuse. In his mind, he had used them, plain and simple.

Recalling his own time in high school, Mark was thankful he had chosen not to fall into that trap. A deep sense of honesty had made such a charade impossible. On the other hand, he'd missed the prom. The traditional male-female pairings that seemed so necessary to the institution had forced him to boycott the event completely. What stung was that afterward, he'd discovered one of his female acquaintances would have been happy to go as just friends, but she'd also skipped the prom because no one had asked her.

"I've fooled around with guys a few times," Cliff plodded on. "Locker room stuff." Falling silent, he paused to consider the experiences. His body had welcomed the release of rutting sex, but otherwise the encounters had disappointed. The exercise had been shallow and empty. The guys he'd been with had been too concerned with preserving their masculinity to permit any sign of real affection. Even then, Cliff had known he needed something more.

The silence lasted for a minute or more before Mark said quietly, "You said you'd been thinking of me before yesterday. What did you mean?"

Cliff turned toward the man sitting on the passenger side of the car and then wished he could see his face. "I noticed you watching me and guessed you were interested." It had been a thrilling realization for Cliff. After the initial surprise, he'd studied the guy. He'd even cautiously allowed himself the fantasy of imagining what it might be like. "I toyed with the idea of talking to you, getting to know you, and maybe even letting things happen. But I knew I would never have the balls to do it."

Mark didn't know what to say. Here was the same sexy football player Mark had watched in class, and it turned out he'd been watching back. It seemed impossible. "Am I really that oblivious?" Mark asked himself aloud.

"Maybe I was just subtle," Cliff offered.

"Apparently more subtle than I was." Mark was still reviewing what Cliff had told him. "So what changed?"

"Yesterday, in the park, when I kissed you, I was worried about you. I couldn't believe it was you I had knocked down. I was afraid I had seriously hurt you." Cliff paused to rein in his racing thoughts. "We were so close. I was touching you. You looked so… vulnerable." Cliff remembered feeling like an observer as his body acted on its own, taking what it wanted. "After I kissed you, I panicked." He stopped talking and closed his eyes.

"You freaked me out pretty good too," Mark said soothingly. "I thought it was all some sort of prank."

Cliff hadn't thought of that. "I'm sorry." He didn't know what else to say.

"Don't be. It's past." Mark wanted to reassure Cliff. He had an idea how difficult this was for him. "Why don't you tell me about this evening?"

The conversation was going better than Cliff had feared. As hard as it was, it felt good to say these things. He resolved to be completely open. "As I got to know you, I discovered you were more than I imagined. I discovered I liked you. The reality was better than the fantasy."

"You had fantasies about me?" Mark teased mischievously. He was beginning to believe what he was hearing. Maybe Cliff really did like him. It felt like Christmas morning, and he had gotten exactly what he wanted. "I'm sorry," he said, realizing too late that he was embarrassing the other man. "I couldn't help it. I mean, this really hot guy is telling me he likes me!"

"I do like you," Cliff said. It felt good to say it out loud.

Mark reached over and placed a hand on Cliff's thigh. "I like you too." Cliff grasped the hand and held it tightly. "What happens now?" Mark asked.

"I don't know," Cliff replied. "I just needed to explain. I hoped… I don't know what I hoped. I just didn't want you to leave."

The admission was astonishing to Mark. A question popped into his head. "I'm not very experienced when it comes to sex," Mark said clumsily. "I don't know if that was what you had in mind by saying you didn't want me to leave." He found it difficult to continue but managed. "I would like to get to know you better."

"I'm not all that experienced either," Cliff said, elated. "You'll have to go easy on me, Bobcat." He squeezed Mark's hand. "Why don't we go to my place and get warmed up?"

"Oh, I haven't heard it called that before." Mark was both terrified and thrilled at the prospect of opening this Christmas present. "On a less romantic note, can we stop somewhere first so I can get a toothbrush?"

Cliff smiled indulgently as he started the car. "Whatever you want, Bobcat."

Chapter 11

MARK insisted on going into the pharmacy alone. He wasn't so helpless that he couldn't manage a simple errand on his own. Besides, Cliff had become excessively affectionate after they'd left the wharf. He wanted to hold Mark's hand and touch his leg. At a stoplight, he leaned over and demanded a kiss. Mark found himself shifting uncomfortably in his seat, trying to accommodate the interest his body was taking in these attentions. He didn't think he could handle the distraction of a randy Cliff in a public place.

After grabbing the first toothbrush he came across, Mark was making for the checkout when he noticed the display of condoms. He stopped in his tracks. *Am I seriously considering that?* Cliff hadn't indicated how far this was going to go. *Oh man, am I that easy?* Mark gave the question some consideration. *Damn, I really am that easy!* He picked up a box nearly at random before he could reconsider and grabbed a little bottle of lube for good measure. Treasures in hand, he sprinted to the checkout. Mark blushed a little at his own presumption as he watched the bored cashier indifferently run his purchases through.

On returning to the car, and even before Mark was settled in the seat, Cliff whined exaggeratedly, "You took forever." Cliff knew he was acting like a big lonely dog waiting for his master. He was so far gone he didn't care.

"My, we are impatient," said Mark again, astonished by the change in the stoic football player he knew from class. "I wasn't gone that long."

"I was afraid you slipped out the back," Cliff teased.

"With you waiting for me, I couldn't get back fast enough." Cliff's open affection warmed Mark. He wondered how long it would last and then chastised himself. *Enjoy it! Don't ask stupid questions.*

The speed at which Cliff drove back to his place was perhaps not entirely legal. Right now, he didn't care. Mark was close behind him as Cliff impatiently worked the lock on the apartment door. Once inside he couldn't wait for them to take off their winter things. He grabbed Mark and pressed him against the wall. He retained just enough presence of mind to be careful of the smaller man's injured arm, but Mark didn't seem to be complaining.

Cliff held Mark's shoulders and kissed his mouth with an almost desperate intensity. He pressed against Mark, pinning him to the wall. His right hand slid up behind Mark's neck while his left hand found its way into Mark's open coat and played across the fabric guarding his chest and stomach. Cliff's tongue touched Mark's tongue. He savored the taste of him. He bit Mark's full bottom lip gently. Oh, how he had wanted to do that. Letting go of the lip he'd kissed, he bit Mark's chin roughly. Momentarily frightened that he had gone too far, he was relieved when he heard a low, throaty sound of pleasure from his bobcat. That sound increased his excitement and lowered his restraints even further. He growled in response.

The assault surprised Mark. He hadn't expected anything like this. He'd never expected to enjoy the rough treatment so much. His erection was now painfully intense. An implacable wall of muscle was holding him in place. He wanted to touch the man. Almost panting, he managed to get out, "Hey y'big moose, you could at least let me get my coat off."

"Too much work," Cliff rasped, going in for another kiss. He pressed his body against the smaller man's, letting him feel the full extent of his excitement.

Even through clothing, there was no mistaking the press of Cliff's cock against Mark's thigh. Mark really needed to be free of some of these clothes. He needed to touch this man, everywhere. Even with two good hands, he knew he was no match for Cliff. He couldn't overpower him, so he would have to persuade him. In a tone between reason and

THE LAST SNOW OF WINTER

seduction, Mark suggested, "I'm sure I could make it worth your while."

The words interrupted Cliff's assault. "Yeah?" The look he gave Mark as he considered the proposition was far different from the usual bold glare he wore for the public. It was almost a look of hunger. Reading it, Mark knew he was probably in over his head but didn't care. Cliff stepped back a pace and shouldered his coat onto the floor. He then bent down to struggle with his bootlaces.

Mark immediately took the opportunity to shed his own coat and toe off his boots. He stepped around Cliff's hunched form to wait. When Cliff straightened, Mark was behind him. As the bigger man turned, Mark backed him into the wall. He ran his free hand up Cliff's chest, leaned in close enough to touch cheeks, and demanded huskily, mouth near Cliff's ear, "Take off your shirt."

Cliff knew he could easily pick up the smaller man, but instead he relented and lifted his shirt over his head. Lust had made him aggressive, too aggressive. It frightened him that he might have hurt the other man. Not that Mark seemed to mind the treatment. Cliff waited expectantly for the next command.

Running his hand over a furry, well-muscled chest and stopping to circle a nipple with a finger, Mark leaned in again and pulled gently at Cliff's thick earlobe with his teeth. He felt the big man shiver as hot breath tickled his ear. Mark dropped his hand to the waistband of Cliff's jeans. One-handed, he expertly unfastened the top button and pushed his palm flat against Cliff's belly. He then slid his fingers down to caress the sensitive skin still hidden by the denim.

Content to allow his little bobcat to take the lead, Cliff watched as Mark unzipped his jeans. With Mark's help, the jeans fell to the floor. He felt a warm hand slide past the elastic of his underwear. Mark was easing them down too. Once free of the elastic, Cliff's cock slapped his stomach. A line of glistening pre-cum connected his belly and cockhead.

Mark nipped at Cliff's chin gently. A reminder of what Cliff had done to him. His hand caressed Cliff's cock and balls. The cock felt hot and heavy in his palm. The big man hummed and gave him another look of longing. Needing no other encouragement, Mark knelt and slid Cliff's underwear further down his legs. The big man's body smelled warmly of soap and spice. The scent clouded Mark's head. He admired the man's cock a moment. Cliff was uncircumcised. Mark had no experience with that novelty. *Later,* he told himself, *you can take a better look at it later.* Mark licked the drop of clear liquid threatening to drip from the cockhead. The pre-cum was slightly sweet. The skin was velvety. He tongued Cliff's balls gently. Cliff's thick cock pressed hot against his cheek. Pulling away, Mark trailed his tongue along the bottom of Cliff's cock from the base to the tip. It jumped from the stimulation. Then in one quick motion, he swallowed the length whole.

Unprepared, the palms of Cliff's hands slapped the wall behind him. His head snapped back, and he drew in a sharp breath. *I didn't expect that!* Mark was mouthing his cock expertly. Taking the length loosely and quickly and then applying gentle suction as he let it back out slowly over and over. After only a few minutes, Cliff seemed to lose the ability to form conscious thoughts. All he knew was that he wouldn't last long. He rasped, "You're going to make me cum."

Mark leaned back and looked up, smiling shamelessly. "I think that was the idea."

This time when Mark took him, Cliff grabbed his head and held him. His cock was deep in Mark's throat. Cliff shuddered and came in rough jerks. He howled. The animal sound was a combination of pain and desire.

Mark swallowed instinctively. When Cliff let him go, he leaned back, gasping and breathing hard to admire the man barely able to stand before him. Mark was pleased. He really wasn't that experienced but had a good imagination and knew his own body well enough to imagine what might feel good to another man. That roar had been a surprise, though. Mark didn't think he could even make that much noise. He hoped no one was home downstairs.

Eyes closed and mind empty, Cliff drifted. *It's a good thing this wall is here to help me stay up.* As his brain began to reengage, he looked down at the man sitting back on his haunches in front of him.

THE LAST SNOW OF WINTER

"Get up here, Bobcat." He reached down to help pull him up. "You've got too many clothes on."

They held each other. Cliff ran his hands up and down Mark's body. The kisses were tender now, not as needy as they had been. Cliff began to undress the smaller man, wanting to feel his bare skin and see his graceful body again. It took some doing, but Cliff managed to get Mark undressed. He insisted gently that Mark had to wear the sling for his arm. To ease Mark's disappointment, he growled suggestively in the smaller man's ear, "Maybe I can return the favor." Cliff grasped Mark's cock and gave it a firm squeeze to ensure the other man understood.

"I'd like that." Mark ran his fingers over the russet fur of Cliff's broad chest. "Maybe you'd like to do something else for me."

"Oh, like what?" Cliff was definitely curious.

"I'd like to feel you inside me." Mark couldn't believe how brazen he was being, but he wanted this, and he was afraid he might not have another chance. He watched as comprehension dawned in Cliff's face. Playing coy, he added, "If you're interested."

A significant part of Cliff's anatomy was interested. He could feel his cock growing heavy again. *Is Mark serious?* Cliff watched his amazing little bobcat for a moment. *He looks serious.* "I've never done that before." Oh yes, he wanted to, but he hesitated. "I'm a pretty big guy."

"Are you bragging?" Mark teased.

"I don't want to hurt you." Cliff knew he had played a little rough earlier. He was thrilled that the other man seemed to enjoy it, but he couldn't hurt him.

"You'll just have to go slow," Mark soothed.

Cliff knew he wanted to but brought up one last concern. "What about being safe?"

Mark reached over and picked up the plastic bag from the pharmacy off the floor where it had fallen. "We'll just have to see if these are your size." He handed the little box to Cliff.

Cliff smiled broadly. "You little hussy!" If it hadn't been for the other man's injury, Cliff would have thrown him over his shoulder and carried him to the bed. As it was, he herded him to the bedroom. Once there, he kissed Mark and then urged him bodily onto the bed.

Lying on his back, Mark watched the naked giant standing at the foot of the bed, practically leering at him. "What're you waiting for, big guy?" Mark's legs were slightly apart, and his cock pointed to the ceiling.

The man was beautiful. Cliff had to take a moment to admire his long, sexy body. He crawled up between the sinewy legs, pushing them even further apart. Cliff couldn't help but stare at Mark's balls. They were larger than his were. The skin was a dusky brown. He licked them. He tried to fit his mouth around them but couldn't. Diverting his attention to Mark's cock, Cliff tried to repeat some of what Mark had done for him. It wasn't as easy as it had looked, but he sure as hell didn't mind trying.

From the sound of it, Mark appreciated Cliff's efforts. He was reluctant to stop, but Cliff was also anxious to feel his cock inside Mark's ass. Not sure how to proceed, he lifted Mark's legs. Mark pulled his knees toward his chest; he was still quite flexible despite the bad arm. Entranced by the reality of what he was about to do, Cliff traced the now exposed opening with a finger. The skin was hot. He grabbed for the condoms. The box didn't cooperate. *Damn it, these should be easier to work!*

Mark had to stop himself from laughing. The look of desperation on Cliff's face made the urge hard to resist. Once Cliff had the condom on, Mark was afraid he would just barge in. In a soothing voice, he cautioned gently, "Don't forget the lube. It will make it easier. Use your fingers to stretch the opening first. It'll be tight."

It was. Cliff greased his cock and his fingers. He then began fingering Mark's hole. When he slipped his finger past the tight muscle of the opening, he couldn't believe how tight it was. *And hot!* He watched as Mark pushed his head back in response to the sensation. *He's gorgeous!* Cliff worked his finger in and out, watching the man's face. He had been afraid that he was going to get all the pleasure out of this. He could see now that Mark wanted it too.

"Add another finger," Mark suggested in a raspy voice.

Cliff did. It was so tight.

When Mark couldn't wait any longer, he breathed, "Now you. Go slow."

Cliff placed the head of his cock against Mark's hole. He pressed. It seemed impossible that he would be able to fit, but the opening stretched around the head of his cock. Mark's ass was yielding. *Oooh, it's so tight!*

Mark groaned and gasped when Cliff's cock pushed past the stretched ring of muscle. He could feel it burn. The man was so big. "Slowly," Mark cautioned. He reminded his own body to relax to be better able to accommodate the intrusion.

The feeling was not what Cliff expected. Mark's flesh was hot around his cock. Cliff ran his hands up the backs of Mark's thighs. He felt the muscles of Mark's legs, watching Mark's face the whole time. Cliff pulled his cock back experimentally, sliding in again slowly, a little deeper this time. *Amazing, I'm inside!* Cliff repeated the motion, in and out. It got easier. In no time, he was sliding in and out without difficulty. He pressed in deep, burying his cock to the balls. He watched as Mark stroked his own cock. Mark threw his head back, exposing his neck. Cliff wanted to kiss it, bite it. The pleasure was building. *Almost!*

Mark listened to Cliff's breathing. It was getting harsher and more ragged. His rhythm was becoming irregular. Mark was close too. He was ready when Cliff roared this time. The animalistic sound pushed him over the edge. Thick, hot liquid splattered his sweaty stomach.

Breathing hard, Cliff pulled out slowly. He felt weak in the knees. He felt weak everywhere. When Cliff was sure he could stand, he slid off the bed and looked down at his spent little bobcat. "I'll be right back," he rumbled softly. Cliff padded to the bathroom to clean up. A few minutes later, he was back with a warm cloth and a towel. He carefully wiped down Mark's body. Clean, he crawled up beside him and kissed him gently, lovingly.

The two men drifted awhile, dozing lightly, exhausted from the activity. Mark's left arm was pinned under Cliff's head. It tingled, but he didn't mind. He caressed the skin he could reach with his fingers.

Cliff stirred."Hi," he said, smiling, looking into his lover's brown eyes.

"Hi." What else was there to say, really? Mark was content. They could just stay this way forever.

"I didn't hurt you, did I?" Cliff asked, no longer smiling.

"I may walk funny for a while," Mark replied, laughing, "but you won't hear me complain." Mark then realized the other man was truly worried. "Relax, I'm fine. I'm a big boy, remember. I can take care of myself." He kissed Cliff on the bridge of his nose. "Um, I do need my arm back, though." Once free, Mark rose and sprinted to the bathroom.

When Mark returned, they kissed and petted for a while but eventually drifted off. Cliff slept close with his hand splayed over Mark's belly, holding him possessively.

Chapter 12

THE angry red numbers floating above the table on Cliff's side of the bed glowed 4:12. Mark had to crane his neck over the bulk of the other man to see the clock. He hated digital clocks. They always seemed to tell him things he didn't want to know. The one in his bedroom at home was constantly telling him "It's time to get up." This one was telling him "You should be sleeping." Mark couldn't sleep. His elbow ached. He hadn't remembered to take anything for the pain before bed.

Mark listened. Cliff was sleeping peacefully beside him. The sound of his breathing was deep and regular. The sound amused Mark. It was almost a snore. He found it comforting somehow. *Weird*, he thought as he considered the idea. Mark had been awake for a while but had no intention of moving. He didn't want to disturb his bedmate. Cliff was warm and safe beside him. No, Mark was staying right here.

Some people never seemed to think, while others found it hard not to. Mark fell into the second group. He found it difficult to suppress a natural tendency to overanalyze. The events of the last two days lay jumbled and scattered across the interior of his mind. He was reviewing, analyzing, and agonizing over all that had happened.

Mark told himself that he didn't regret what he and Cliff had done, but he knew that wasn't entirely true. He had always imagined sex to be a part of love and a relationship. He worried that Cliff might think he was some sort of slut who slept around. He also worried that this might be the only time for them. *You're being stupid*, he told himself. *You knew what you wanted and you got it. You had one night. What more do you want?* Mark knew he needed more.

As a teen coming to terms with his sexuality, Mark had once faced a very difficult decision. In the end, he'd made a choice by asking himself, "If you're willing to give up everything, what risks would you dare to take instead?" He considered the situation he was in now. Applying the same formula crystallized his disorganized thoughts into order. *Do you want to keep fooling around with Cliff? Yes, if the man is willing, I want it. What if he doesn't want a relationship? Would you continue seeing him just for sex?* Right then, with the beefy bear sleeping right next to him, Mark had to admit he would. In the light of day, he wasn't sure how he would feel. Mark also wanted a future. *Then you need to find out and decide*, his inner-self determined coolly.

Mark turned his head to watch the sleeping form beside him. The massive football player looked so beautiful to his eyes. He resisted the urge to caress Cliff's cheek. The sound of his breathing was soothing. The heat from his body comforted Mark. He could feel himself falling asleep. He could also feel himself falling for this man. *Crap!*

Cliff woke at his usual time for a Sunday morning. He was an early riser as a rule. It was a pleasure to wake up this morning and find his little bobcat sleeping peacefully beside him. He remembered the fun of the night before. He was tempted to wake Mark up and see if he wanted to have another go. *No, I don't want him to think I only lust after him for sex.* He watched the sleeping man for a few more seconds. An idea popped into his head, unexpected but fully formed. *Yeah, there's a plan*, he agreed with himself. He wanted to do something nice for his frisky lover. Cliff slipped out of bed as lightly and quietly as he could, grabbed his clothes from the floor and crept out of the room.

Dressing silently in the still darkened living room, Cliff considered where he could go. He had decided to put together a romantic breakfast for the two of them, but his fridge was sadly bare. It was Sunday morning too. That would be a problem. He should have picked up more supplies at the grocery store the day before. *Of course, you didn't know then you would need them*, he reasoned happily. Inspiration came. *Yes, the convenience store downtown would be open.* He dressed for outdoors, found his keys, and quietly opened the door.

THE LAST SNOW OF WINTER

The selection available at the convenience store was disappointing. Cliff's hopes of finding supplies for a perfect, lazy breakfast in bed were fading. In the end, he picked up a newspaper, a bottle of orange juice, a half-dozen blueberry muffins, and a pair of very ripe bananas. It wasn't much, but it would have to do. He ran back home, hoping that Mark would still be asleep.

Cliff quietly opened the door to his apartment. The living room was dark as the blinds were still drawn. He held his breath and listened for a few seconds, but the place was silent. Pleased that his plan was going so well, Cliff pulled off his boots and coat and noiselessly crept to the kitchen to prepare.

Mark woke suddenly from the most wonderful dream. He rarely remembered his dreams. He didn't this time either, but he knew it had been a good one. It put him in a happy mood. The room was bright with light. He looked around to find a shape he took to be Cliff standing by the window. The blind was open and sunlight flooded in.

"Wake up, sleepyhead." The voice rang out powerfully loud. Mark groaned and closed his eyes. Cliff placed a glass of orange juice next to another on the table by the bed. He smiled at his bobcat and then leaned over to give him a kiss. He stroked Mark's cheek lightly. "Were you planning to sleep all day?"

Eyes open, it took a moment for Mark's vision to adjust to the change in lighting. He focused on the face of his lover from the night before. Cliff had that radiant, joyous look again. Mark had to admire it. "You know, if other people saw that look on your face right now, they would all fall in love with you instead of being terrified."

Cliff laughed. "You're full of shit."

"Oh no, you could make anyone love you with that look of yours," Mark told him.

"Well, I only look this way at you." Cliff got up to get the rest of their breakfast from the kitchen. "Stay here, and I'll get some food." He considered what Mark had just told him. *He's just messing with you*, he assured himself. The exchange pleased him, though.

Mark watched the man go. He shifted into a sitting position with his back against the headboard. The air and the headboard were cool on his bare skin. Well, here he was. Morning had come, and he still wanted to stay with Cliff. They would have to talk soon, Mark was certain. He needed to know where he stood. *Besides, it's not like you're the sort to leave well enough alone.*

Cliff returned to the bedroom carrying a cookie sheet laden with the items he had collected. The cookie sheet was the closest thing he had to a serving tray. It was too small for the job but it performed the task well enough. Cliff had carried in the glasses of juice separately, not trusting the flimsy metal pan. He placed the makeshift tray carefully on the bed beside Mark and then stood back to observe the other man's reaction.

The production was a surprise for Mark. He would never have guessed that the burly, reserved, fierce football player he watched in class had such a soft side. He looked up from the tray to the man standing and waiting by the bed. "Well, knock me over with a feather. You're a romantic?" Mark allowed his surprise at the realization to sound in his voice and show on his face. He smiled broadly. "Who would have guessed?"

The big man placed a hand over his heart as if the accusation hurt. Cliff was pleased that he had made his bobcat happy. He crawled up next to him on the bed. Between the two of them, there was little room for the tray. Cliff leaned over to demand a kiss in reward for his thoughtfulness.

One kiss turned to three. Mark didn't want to leave, but his body had its own needs. He excused himself and promised to be right back. Bladder seen to, Mark took the time to wash his face and brush his teeth before returning. *No need to subject the poor guy to more morning breath,* he reasoned. Mark found Cliff waiting patiently in bed. He had taken off his shirt and sat with the comforter pulled up over his hips. Mark studied him for a moment from the door.

"I like the view," Cliff announced when he noticed Mark standing there naked, framed by the doorway. Mark hadn't bothered to put anything on for his jaunt to the bathroom. Cliff's gaze ran over Mark's body like a physical caress. He enjoyed the long, graceful lines of the man's body. Mark shivered pleasantly in reaction to the scrutiny. Throwing back the covers, Cliff patted the bed, indicating that Mark should join him.

Under the covers, the bed was still warm. The warmth was welcome. Mark's feet had gone cold on the bare floor. He snuggled in close to the big man, who put his arm around his waist to pull him closer. Mark's good arm was pinned between their bodies now. He leaned his head against Cliff's shoulder. Cliff placed his chin on top of Mark's head. They stayed this way for a few minutes, just holding each other. Then Cliff's stomach interrupted the moment with a noisy growl.

Mark laughed. "Time to feed the bear," he announced loudly to the room. They separated and repositioned themselves to make it easier to eat. Cliff handed Mark a glass of orange juice. The muffins were dry and the bananas mushy. It didn't matter. The two men read the paper and enjoyed each other's company. It felt familiar and comfortable.

There was very little conflict while they read the paper together. They traded sections back and forth but rarely competed in their interests. In the end, Mark favored the comics and Cliff wanted the sports section. After finishing the funnies, Mark watched as Cliff poured over the sports stats.

When Cliff finally set aside the paper, Mark said, "Thank you for all this. It's really sweet." Mark watched as the other man uncomfortably shrugged off his thanks and busied himself with searching through the paper again. "It's too late." Mark went on, "I already know that beneath that big, tough, football player exterior is a squishy teddy bear."

Cliff stopped evading. He looked to Mark, let out a breath, and replied, "You're welcome."

Mark considered his friend and then said jokingly, "Don't worry, I won't tell anyone."

That brought a small chuckle from the big man. Cliff reached out and took Mark's hand. "I guess I am a little guarded in public." Cliff had to admit it felt good to let his guard down. At least while he was with Mark. It felt so natural when he was alone with his little bobcat.

This seemed as good a time as any to get a few things out in the open, Mark decided. He took a breath and started with, "I need to ask you something. I'm afraid that I'm going to mess this all up, but I need to know."

"That sounds ominous," Cliff replied. He squeezed the hand he was still holding in encouragement. "Go ahead."

"I've had a really great time with you the last two days. I mean, except for the broken arm." Mark knew he was resorting to humor to ease his own discomfort. He continued, "And the head injury, which I don't really remember." He frowned and creased his brow as if in confusion. Cliff laughed. More serious now, he added, "Anyway, I guess I want to know if I'll be able to see you again."

Cliff considered the question Mark was voicing. He figured he had a good idea about the unasked questions too. After some thought, he said, "I've really enjoyed the time we've spent together." Playing Mark's game of using humor to lighten the serious nature of the exchange, he complained, "I'm a little disappointed that the sex didn't even get mentioned. You know, I thought it was pretty good." He winked and smiled at Mark.

"Yeah, I guess it was pretty good," Mark replied flatly.

"Good? It was hot!" Cliff clarified with enthusiasm. Turning sober, he said frankly, "I want to see you again." After a beat, he asked, "Now, what do you mean by seeing each other? Do you mean sex? Or are you thinking dating? Tell me." Having asked the question that Mark hadn't, Cliff waited to see what the other man would say. Cliff knew this was important for both of them. He just wasn't sure how they would work it out.

"I've never dated before." Mark exhaled slowly. "I can't even imagine how dating would work for us." Mark didn't want to cause problems for Cliff. He knew people would notice if they were together. "I would like for us to be friends. It would be nice if it went further than that." It was time to be honest. "I want to continue having sex with you, but I need us to be more than… fuck buddies." Mark winced and dropped his gaze to stare at the pattern printed on the comforter. There it was, out in the open.

"What if I want the same thing?" Cliff said straightforwardly in response.

Mark looked at him. It was what he wanted to hear, but he could barely believe it. There was a lump in his throat. He had been afraid that Cliff would make a different choice.

Cliff pulled Mark close and hugged him clumsily. He kissed him and pressed his forehead against Mark's. "We'll have to be careful," he stated for both of them.

Having come this far, Mark needed to go all the way. He wanted all his fears exposed. It was the only way he would be able to face them. "How are we going to pass me off as anything but your gay friend? Seriously, people will look at me and go 'Gay'!"

"I don't believe that." While Cliff was doing his best to minimize the other man's fears and calm him down, he had to admit that a small part of him worried that maybe Mark was right. *So, what then?* "Look, are you trying to make me say this is a bad idea?" Cliff's tone was stern bordering on angry.

The anger in the other man's voice helped focus Mark's thinking. "I'm afraid I might hurt you. Without meaning to, I could ruin your chances for a career." Mark saw that Cliff was about to say something. He held up his hand as a sign to wait. There was more. Mark plodded on, "I'm afraid… that you would blame me."

Cliff finally understood. He opened his mouth to say what he had planned to say in comfort, but he couldn't. It wasn't good enough to just comfort. He needed to be honest. "I don't know what the future will bring. Anything might happen."

"I know," Mark replied quickly. "I just needed to say it."

"We'll do this together. If we get caught, we'll deal with it together." Cliff looked to Mark. "Agreed?"

"Okay." Mark felt drained. He pushed his worries aside and glanced at the man sitting next to him on the bed. He felt the need to lighten the mood again. "So, if we're going to try dating, do I have to bring you flowers?"

Cliff laughed loudly. The tension was broken. He felt lighter. "Yes, I think you need to give me flowers." Thinking better of it, he asked, "You're not going to embarrass me, are you?"

"Oh yes, but only in private." *It's going to be all right*, Mark realized. They were going to be all right.

Chapter 13

IF ONLY it were possible to stay in bed forever. Cliff was content to give himself the morning off. After their conversation earlier, he knew they both needed this time to wind down. He watched Mark, who was dozing lightly beside him. Mark had confessed that he'd been awake most of the night worrying. As he watched, a voice in his head asked: *Do you know what you're getting yourself into?*

No, he answered the voice truthfully. Cliff wasn't worried.

A dozen tasks whispered for his attention. Chapters to read, papers to write, laundry to do. He hadn't gone to the gym to work out the day before like he usually did. It wasn't too hard to drown out the whisperings. None of it seemed as important as staying here and watching over his little bobcat. It could all wait.

The light in the room changed abruptly. The passage of a cloud temporarily dimmed the brilliant sunlight. In the relative shadow, the air felt noticeably cooler. Cliff saw that it was almost eleven. Maybe he should have a shower while Mark slept. Light flooded the room again. The cloud had passed. Cliff looked back to watch Mark sleep and found him with his eyes open.

"Hey," Mark said to the man sitting beside him on the bed. Rested now, he shook off the remnants of embarrassment he felt at how he had panicked earlier. From now on, he was determined to relax and let things unfold as they would.

"Hey yourself," Cliff responded. "I should probably warn you. I'm a morning person."

"I'm not usually in bed this late." Mark considered the implications of the simple assertion. *Other mornings together?* He sat up and brushed his fingers along the bare skin of Cliff's forearm. Fine golden hairs glistened in the light from the window. "I've been having trouble sleeping," he said without emphasis.

"You worry too much, Bobcat." Cliff's tone was gently recriminating.

There was no point in arguing. Mark knew he was right.

Feeling the need to change the subject, Cliff asked, "Do you want to jump in the shower first?"

Mark considered it. A thought came of itself, and in response, a smile played across his features.

Seeing the smile, Cliff creased his brow. "Where did that wicked look come from?" he asked half seriously.

Assuming an air of innocence, Mark explained, "Well, I was just thinking that you could give me a hand. You know, help me clean the hard-to-reach places." Mark nearly batted his lashes. He would have liked to but didn't think he could pull it off. In the end, his attitude and the suggestion were enough to have the effect he wanted.

Cliff was momentarily taken aback but caught himself and played naive. "You managed to shower all by yourself yesterday," he suggested innocently. "You didn't need any help then." The image of Mark in the shower was there for his mind's eye to see. He liked the idea.

"I didn't know you were interested in helping yesterday," Mark replied, raising his eyebrows.

"Who says I'm interested in helping?" Cliff said huffily.

Mark slipped his hand onto the other man's lap. Cliff's interest was causing a telltale tent to form in the comforter there. Mark patted the bulging fabric. "Well, if you're not interested." He made to crawl off the bed.

THE LAST SNOW OF WINTER

Cliff grabbed the other man by the waist and pulled him back. "You are going to drive me crazy. You know that?" The smile Mark gave him was luminous. It warmed Cliff's heart. He needed time to take it in. "You are so lucky you have that broken arm. It's the only thing that keeps me from jumping you all the time."

Mark laughed at that. "Don't think I don't know it. Come on, Teddy Bear. Haven't you ever wanted to shower with another man?"

"I shower with men all the time, a dozen or so at once," Cliff joked. "It's not as much fun as you might think." Maybe he had just done it so many times that it didn't mean anything. Showering with the guys in the locker room wasn't a big deal for Cliff. This would be different, though, he knew. It would be his beautiful little bobcat under the hot water.

"Maybe I can make it worth your while." Mark jumped off the bed. His erection was visible now. He stopped at the doorway, turning to see what Cliff would do.

Cliff watched the long, lean muscles of Mark's body move and flex under smooth skin. He slowly crawled off the bed and stalked toward him like a predator. Cliff had half-expected Mark to make a run for the bathroom like a high-strung cat. Mark didn't. He stood his ground and waited. Cliff took him in his arms. Their erections rubbed together as he held and kissed the man who was quickly becoming an essential part of his life.

"Come on, Teddy Bear," Mark said with a smile, the words obscured by Cliff's lips still pressed to his own. "You can wash my back."

"Get on with you." Cliff let Mark loose and patted the smaller man's ass roughly to encourage him toward the bathroom.

Mark adjusted the water as Cliff stood by watching. Satisfied with the temperature, he stepped into the shower, reaching out to pull Cliff in too. Cliff felt almost hypnotized by the smaller man as Mark directed him to stand under the spray. Rivulets of water coursed over Cliff's body. Entranced by the sight, Mark told him reverently in a barely audible whisper, "You're so beautiful." Mark saw Cliff lower his eyes at the compliment. He read the other man's expression and said, "You don't believe me."

"I think you're biased." Cliff didn't meet Mark's eye. He knew he wasn't beautiful. He was an ugly lump of a man.

"I assure you, my ass is completely gay. Women need not apply," Mark assured. He reached for a bar of soap and started rubbing it across Cliff's well-muscled chest. "I don't think I'm the only one with self-esteem issues." Mark continued lathering the body standing before him.

"I'm not beautiful," Cliff stated flatly. "There's no use pretending."

"Well, I could say you're… imposing," Mark suggested with consideration. He took a step back to assess the man blatantly. "Rugged," he amended. Mark put his hand to his chin in an obvious show of thought and added, "Powerfully built." Mark finally breathed out and said with some heat, "Sexy as all get out."

Cliff looked down and shook his head but smiled a little.

"But then I would only be talking about the outside." Mark was serious now. "I think you're beautiful on the inside too." He resumed lathering Cliff's body. "And I'm never wrong," he affirmed with humor in his voice.

"Okay, Bobcat." Cliff looked to the man who was happily rubbing him down. "Let's say I told you that I think you are the most beautiful man I've ever seen. How would you respond?"

"Well, that's just silly." Mark pointedly didn't meet Cliff's eye now. "There are some seriously hot guys out there."

"Ha!" Cliff crossed his arms in satisfaction.

Caught and knowing it, what could Mark do? "Fine, I will accept that you find me adorable if you allow that I find you beautiful in both body and spirit." He motioned Cliff to turn around in the flow of water and began applying lather to his broad back. Mark only wished he had the use of both his hands.

Figuring it was best to just let it go, Cliff said instead, "I thought I was supposed to be helping you." Not that he was complaining. The sensation of Mark massaging his slippery skin was wonderful. He felt the other man press his body close against his back. Mark's hard cock slid along his soapy ass.

Standing on his toes to bring his mouth close to Cliff's ear, Mark purred, "I just wanted an excuse to feel you all over."

Months ago, when Cliff had first fantasized about what it might be like to be with a guy like Mark, he hadn't imagined anything like this. The Mark of his imagination had been an abstract construction. The things he'd pictured them doing together were similar to the things he had done with guys before, perhaps with less fear. However, this Mark was different. He was creative, quirky, sensitive, and passionate. Cliff enjoyed his touch and reveled in the interest Mark showed in him.

Cliff turned to face Mark. He pulled him close, held him with one arm, and used his other hand to hold and rub their two cocks together. Mark kissed Cliff's neck and nipped at his earlobe. Water coursed over their bodies, creating serpentine patterns in the hair of their chests. Cliff was surprised to find he was breathing hard. The elevated state of arousal had crept up on him. Even in the overheated air of the shower, Mark's breath was hot on his neck. The smaller man was holding him tightly with one arm. Cliff noticed the flush of Mark's skin and heard him almost panting in the heat. Cliff's excitement increased with the knowledge that he was pleasing his bobcat. When Mark began to spasm, Cliff felt himself let go too. He bellowed loudly as he came.

Time passed. Cliff felt weak. The hot water and the excitement had overheated his body. Cliff could tell Mark was feeling the effects too. He could feel him sway and sag a little in his arms. Cliff held him tightly and turned to adjust the water temperature slightly cooler. Then he guided Mark to stand under the flow and began to wash him. The kiss Mark offered in return for the attention was tender.

They didn't speak again until they were back in the bedroom dressing. The silence wasn't awkward. It felt comfortable. They touched each other occasionally, casual contact, while they toweled dry. Cliff was almost reluctant to break the pleasant spell that had fallen over them. Finally, he asked, "What have you got planned for today?"

"I should go home and do my laundry," Mark answered. He was unhappy about wearing the same underwear from the day before. Plus, if he was going to catch the train the next day, he would need clean clothes. The thought made him uncomfortable. He hadn't told Cliff he was planning to leave Monday. Right now, he wanted to stay, but Cliff probably had his own plans for the week.

"I was thinking I might hit the gym for a workout." It wasn't what he wanted to say. Cliff didn't want to appear clingy, but he really wanted to spend more time with Mark. He compromised by asking, "Would you like to have supper with me?"

Pleased by the invitation, Mark replied, "You've done so much for me. Maybe I could make supper for you."

Cliff grinned at the idea. "Not to sound ungrateful, but how do you plan to manage that with one arm?"

Mark opened his mouth to reply but realized Cliff was right. "I guess I hadn't thought of that."

Amused by the look on Mark's face, Cliff took pity and offered, "What if I came by a little early to help?"

"I'd like that." Mark was looking forward to it already.

Chapter 14

NOT wanting Mark to walk home alone, Cliff offered to drop him off before driving himself to the gym. He wasn't really surprised when Mark politely declined the offer, but he allowed his disappointment to sound in his voice as he chastised Mark for still resisting his offers of assistance. "We're supposed to be friends. You're supposed to let me help you."

Initially annoyed by the accusation, Mark calmed himself and explained, "I appreciate your help, but I like the walk. It isn't that far, and I'm perfectly capable." He took a calming breath and said reasonably, "Thank you for watching out for me. I'll be fine."

"Sorry." Cliff's tone was subdued. He wanted to say more but wasn't sure how to proceed. Everything he wanted to say seemed to assume too much. They barely knew each other, but he was acting as if they were in a long-standing relationship. He was sure it was too soon, but it didn't feel that way.

The car forgotten, they walked to the corner together. Mark studied Cliff covertly. *Something's up. He's being too quiet.* The expression that played over Cliff's features didn't reveal any insights to Mark. Sometimes he seemed to be able to read the man fairly well. Right then, he couldn't even imagine what Cliff might be thinking. *Should I ask?* Before he reached a decision, Cliff appeared to shake off whatever it was that was troubling him, and his features took on the expression he wore to class every day.

On reaching the corner where they would part and go their separate ways, Cliff said, "I'll come by around four thirty?" He made an effort to sound casual.

"That sounds great," Mark answered. "I'll see you then."

Not sure how to take his leave, Cliff muttered uncomfortably, "Bye." He then turned and walked away. He burned with the need to do or say more but couldn't think of the proper way. A hug or a kiss was out of the question. Everything else was inadequate. He felt foolish in his indecision. *You've only known each other two days*, he reminded himself. It felt much longer.

Mark watched the man's back for a full minute as he walked away. Something was off. He couldn't determine what it was, but Cliff was different, unreadable. Mark reminded himself that he didn't know Cliff that well yet. *It may be nothing.* Turning for home, he considered what had passed. He thought about it for some time but couldn't come up with a satisfactory explanation for the change in the other man's behavior. *Maybe the difference was just that we were in public.* Faced with a problem without a ready solution, Mark did what he had learned to do from experience. *Let it go*, he told himself. *The answer will come in its own time. There's no use in trying to chase it down.*

The scenery passed by without making much of an impression on Mark. He was barely aware of the passage of time. Usually he studied the familiar surroundings, never failing to find something interesting or some new detail in what he observed. Today his gaze drifted over the houses and trees without taking them in. He smiled absently without being aware of it and spent the time reflecting happily on the unexpected events of the last two days. It seemed like someone else's life. *There's no way I just spent the night with the hot football player from class.*

The laundry was still there when Mark got home. He sighed and then found a box of detergent and collected coins for the machines. Placing it all in the overstuffed basket so he could carry everything under his good arm, Mark stepped to the front door and stopped. Facing the closed door, the logistics of the normally simple chore of doing laundry finally occurred to him. This was going to be a pain, he realized. Grumbling but determined, he set the basket down so he could turn the knob.

Cliff had been working out on the exercise equipment for a while. He preferred free weights, but since there was no one else around today, and he didn't have a spotter, he resigned himself to using the machines instead. Muscles ached pleasantly from the repetitions, but Cliff was finding it hard to keep his focus. He usually worked himself harder than this.

It's a good thing no one is around today, Cliff thought. He had several times caught himself staring blankly into space not moving a muscle. *I must look like an idiot*, he thought. He couldn't help it. Everything reminded him of Mark. He wondered what he was doing now. *Probably something he shouldn't be doing*. The idea brought a smile to his face. That was his little bobcat.

Their parting earlier had left Cliff unsatisfied. He wished he had done more, not just walked away. If Mark had been his girlfriend, Cliff knew he would have hugged and kissed him goodbye right there on the street. It would have been a completely inappropriate show of public affection. Mark would have been embarrassed and pushed him off, but deep down Cliff knew he would have loved it.

Cliff caught himself staring and smiling goofily again. He shook his head to clear the cobwebs. It rankled that he couldn't have that. Straight couples could make out at the mall, but he had to hold back on an empty street. His brain reasoned that it was pointless to whine. *Society isn't ready for two guys kissing on a street corner*. Cliff knew better. Society hadn't stopped him from showing Mark some outward sign of affection. He'd stopped himself.

Progress with the laundry was slow, but Mark plodded on. Everything took at least twice as long, though. After washing the dirty clothes from the week, he stripped the bed to clean the sheets. *Just in case*, he hoped. Folding the clean clothes turned out to be a completely pointless endeavor. Mark did the best he could before eventually giving up.

Not long after that, Mark found himself rooting through the freezer looking for something he could make for supper. He hadn't bought groceries since he wasn't planning to be here for the week. Had the store been open, he would have stopped there before coming home. *So now what?* His hand touched a faded ice cream container. Remembering, he extracted it.

The container was heavy for its size; there obviously wasn't ice cream inside. Mark had completely forgotten about it. The container had been there since the last time his parents had visited. It held some of his mother's homemade rappie pie. Mark had saved it for a treat. He hefted the container and considered. Cliff seemed brave. At worst, they could always order pizza. Mark placed the plastic container in the sink to thaw.

Cliff stood looking at his reflection in the bathroom mirror. After his workout, he had walked home and tried unsuccessfully to concentrate on reading some course material. It was a waste of time. His eyes skimmed the words without retaining the information. He didn't seem to be able to focus his attention on what he was doing. Now, here he was, showered and shaved with an hour to go before he could even consider walking to Mark's place.

This feels like a date. Cliff wasn't really sure. He didn't have much experience with dating, but he imagined this was what it would feel like. Wearing just socks and underwear, Cliff found himself standing in front of his closet, looking at his clothes. Well, he corrected himself, giving his head a shake, he was looking toward his clothes but was daydreaming again. He pulled a dark button-up shirt off a hanger. It was a deep cobalt blue. People said the color looked good on him. Khaki pants and a belt completed the outfit.

Cliff checked himself in the mirror. *Not bad*, he figured. The bottle of cologne his sister had given him at Christmas stood out on the dresser. Cliff had never used it and only kept the gift to be polite. It had been a well-meaning but misguided hint from his sister that she was worried he was never going to settle down and find a nice girl. *What the hell*, he reasoned as he reached for the bottle. *You're this far gone, why not go all the way?*

Time dragged. Cliff sat on the edge of the couch. He tried to distract himself by reading a chapter or two before he left for Mark's place. The effort was again wasted. He didn't remember anything he read. He looked at his watch so frequently that the hands appeared to be not moving at all. Unable to wait any longer, he stood and dressed for the walk. If he walked slowly, he decided, he wouldn't show up too early. *You loser*, he chided himself good-naturedly.

The weather was pleasant enough for the walk. Cliff wasn't an avid walker. He wasn't used to being alone with his thoughts like this. Not that he didn't spend time alone. He just usually kept himself busy enough that his thoughts didn't intrude so much. Classes kept his free time full with reading. Football ate up much of his time, too, during the season. Then there was training. It was easy enough to fill up the days.

The day had progressed into a fine afternoon. Long shadows of branches drew abstract patterns on canvases of undisturbed snow. Cliff tried to imagine how Mark would see them. Far too soon, he was standing next to a row of little white cottages. Cliff looked at his watch and groaned. It wasn't even four yet. He was very early. *Nothing for it*, he reasoned. Walking to the door, he knocked resolutely.

The sharp rap on the door surprised Mark. He looked at the clock on the wall of the kitchen. It was too soon for Cliff to arrive. Walking into the living room, Mark could see the man himself through the glass in the door. Butterflies fluttered in his stomach as he reached for the knob to let him in.

Self-consciously keeping an eye on the neighboring windows, Cliff heard rather than saw the door open beside him. His first sight of Mark was a welcome surprise. His friend stood there in the doorway, barefoot, wearing shorts and a button-up short-sleeved shirt. Buttons undone, the shirt hung open. *Am I staring?* Cliff wondered. The glimpse of a flat, lightly furred belly seemed to excite him more than it should, considering he was intimately familiar with the man standing here. It occurred to him that it must be true that a suggestion of skin is better able to captivate the imagination. *Damn, I'm daydreaming again.*

"Welcome!" Mark said in a cheerful greeting to compensate for his nervousness. "Come in." He stood back to let the man enter.

"I like your outfit. I didn't know dinner was casual," Cliff commented. At least Mark didn't seem bothered by his early arrival.

"It was all I could manage on my own," Mark explained, looking down at himself. "I guess I need your help after all." He smiled. "I'm glad you're here. Can I take your coat?"

Cliff slipped off his coat and handed it over.

Mark stood stock still for a moment. The man had dressed up for him. "You look great! Now I feel underdressed."

"I like the way you're dressed." Cliff wanted to touch but didn't have the courage to do so. He bent to untie his boots instead.

Not being able to manage a hanger, Mark folded Cliff's heavy leather coat over the back of a chair. He turned back to watch the man slip his boots off by the door. "Is it too early to ask for a kiss?"

Cliff broke into a broad smile. "C'mere, Bobcat." He opened his arms and waited as the other man walked into them. Holding Mark tightly, he kissed him deeply. After the kiss, he didn't let go. "I missed you."

"I missed you too," Mark admitted easily. It hardly seemed possible that they were still just getting to know each other.

Dropping his chin on Mark's shoulder, Cliff confessed, "I was miserable when I walked away from you earlier."

"Oh, why?" Mark asked with surprise.

"I wanted to let you know… that I cared." There was no point in denying the fact, not to Mark anyway. Cliff didn't want to spend another afternoon like the one today. "I wanted to grab you and hold you… and show you."

"It would have been quite a show." The mental picture amused Mark. He massaged the back of the larger man's neck with his good hand. Cliff didn't say anything more. "Why don't you show me now?" It came out in a suggestive whisper.

A low rumbling growl issued from deep inside the big man's chest. Cliff quickly turned Mark and pressed against him, pinning him

THE LAST SNOW OF WINTER

to the wall with his own body. Their lips pushed hotly together. The kiss was devouring in its intensity. His arm caught again, Mark grunted involuntarily. Noticing, Cliff eased up the attack and opened a space between them.

"That would have been quite an eyeful for Main Street," Mark said, feeling a little lightheaded.

"Sorry," Cliff mumbled. Without meaning to, he kept hurting Mark.

Now that they were in private again, Mark seemed to be better able to read Cliff's expressions and body language. "Relax," he said. "I'm not complaining."

Cliff nodded his acceptance of what Mark had said but didn't comment.

Mark waited a few seconds and then changed the subject by asking, "Are you willing to give me a hand with supper?"

"Sure. That's why I came early." Cliff made an effort to sound cheerful.

"You look so good. I hate to ask you to help. I don't want you to get dirty." Mark led the way to the kitchen. Cliff followed along silently. "There isn't that much to do." Mark picked up a bowl of apples and turned to face Cliff. The man was standing just inside the doorway but was obviously in another world. Mark placed the bowl on the table. Something was definitely on the big guy's mind. Mark was beginning to feel lost again. He needed to do something.

The kitchen was quite rustic. It looked like a farm kitchen to Cliff. He hadn't seen this room when he'd been here last. It was a smallish space with a chrome-legged, laminate-topped table in the middle. Four chairs clustered around the table. A fridge stood in one corner next to the stove. A white porcelain sink and sideboard were opposite. Cliff suspected he was taking in these details to keep his mind off how he was feeling.

"Can you peel six or so of these?" Mark indicated the bowl, which held apples. Cliff pulled out a chair and sat down. Mark found a paring knife and a baking dish and placed them on the table in front of Cliff. Not sure if this would work or even if it was a good idea, Mark leaned back against the counter and said, "Can I ask you a question?"

"Shoot," Cliff replied automatically, looking up at Mark.

"Why do you want to help me?" Mark asked, keeping his eye on the apple in Cliff's hand.

As Cliff thought about the question, he turned the bright green apple over in his hands. "You're not talking about helping with supper?"

"No," Mark admitted.

"I told you. I'm your friend." Cliff then added, "And I care about you."

Mark nodded his head, listening to the words he had expected to hear. "Can I ask a favor?"

"Of course," Cliff again answered automatically.

Not waiting for the agreement to be qualified, Mark immediately asked, "Can you tell me what's on your mind?" Mark's voice was careful, calculated. "I would like to help if I can. It's only fair." He finished the statement with a shy, sly smile.

He had to laugh. Cliff hadn't even seen it coming. "Nice set-up, you bugger." He laughed again. "All right, Bobcat, I'll try." It wasn't easy for him to articulate. *What is the problem?* He thought about it for a few minutes.

Mark stood by quietly and waited.

"I don't know how to be with you." It wasn't what Cliff had meant to say, but it was what came out. *Was that the real problem?* Perhaps, but he had to admit there was more. He continued speaking, his voice thoughtful, "I'm afraid I'll hurt you, like I did at the door. I got carried away...." His voice trailed off.

"Is that all?" Mark had feared worse. "You didn't hurt me." Seeing Cliff raise his eyebrows at that, he added with a tinge of annoyance, "Not seriously, nothing I'm going to complain about. Look,

Cliff, I'm not that fragile. You're not going to break me." Mark considered the man sitting there and still rolling the apple in his hand. "Are you afraid that if you let go of your self-restraint, you might go too far?"

"Yes. No. I don't know." His brain felt like concrete.

"I trust you." Mark's voice was almost a whisper.

Cliff couldn't look up. "I get so excited when I'm alone with you. I get carried away. Then, when we're in public, I feel myself wanting to do things I shouldn't. Touch you. Kiss you. I want you to know that I...." He couldn't say it.

Mark waited, but Cliff didn't offer any more. "I have a suggestion." Cliff looked up and met his eye. "Loosen the restraints. Let yourself breathe a little. When we're alone, do what you want to do. I trust you." He trusted the big man completely. "When we're in public, I'll know you still care, even if you can't show me right there. Besides"—Mark couldn't help the grin that formed on his face—"if you keep holding back, you're going to run at me like a bull moose in heat every time we're alone."

The laugh came easily. "I'll try," Cliff said in response to the suggestion.

"You do that." Mark hoped he would. "Peel a half dozen of those and then slice them into the dish. Thank you, by the way."

"You're welcome," Cliff replied as he started curling the shiny green peel expertly off the apple in a continuous spiral. "What are we making, anyway?"

"Apple crisp," Mark informed. "I hope you like it. And I was thanking you for opening up."

"Oh. I guess I do keep the reins on pretty tight." Cliff felt exposed, but instead of it making him feel vulnerable, as he would have expected, he felt relieved. Mark seemed to be able to walk past every one of his self-imposed protective barriers effortlessly, stealing in like a cat. Without warning, there he was right next to his heart.

Cliff watched Mark mix dry ingredients into a heavy yellow stoneware bowl. The bowl was bigger than necessary for the contents, but the weight seemed to keep it from moving around as he cut margarine into the mixture. Cliff was impressed at how expertly Mark worked with his left hand and said so. "I thought you were right-handed."

Mark looked up, surprised. "I am." He looked back to his left hand, still in the bowl. "I can do almost anything equally well with both hands except writing."

With Cliff's help, Mark finished preparing their dessert. The dish went into the hot oven, and Mark set the timer. Looking at the clock, he decided it would be a good time to start the main course. "I'm not sure if you're up for this." Mark lifted the ice cream container from the sink.

"Ice cream?" Cliff asked, puzzled.

"No, my mother reuses plastic food containers instead of using Tupperware. I have to say, I respect her for the commitment to recycling, but seriously, I don't think she trusts me with her good Tupperware. It's an Acadian dish called rappie pie." Mark handed the container to Cliff, indicating he should open it. He placed a large cast iron frying pan on the stove in preparation.

Cliff opened the container and looked inside. It didn't look like any food he recognized, but the contents smelled good. He handed it back to Mark. "I'm willing to try anything."

Mark arched his eyebrows wickedly. "Really? I'll keep that in mind." He cut a little margarine into the pan.

"That's not what I meant." Cliff's words and tone were a study in wounded innocence. He enjoyed the banter.

"It's just too bad I left the condoms at your place," Mark teased.

"Actually, they're in my coat pocket," Cliff admitted.

"My, weren't we being hopeful?" Mark moved to stand well within the other man's personal space.

THE LAST SNOW OF WINTER

"I just noticed you forgot them and thought I would be nice and return them to you." Cliff gave the statement an air of simple, honest practicality. He then put his arms around Mark and pulled him closer. "You are going to drive me crazy, Bobcat."

Mark snuggled in and whispered the words directly into Cliff's ear. "You love it."

"I love you." The words came easily.

Mark pulled back and just stared at the man. Had he really heard that? He could feel his chest swell with joy and compress with fear.

"It's probably too soon, but that's how I feel," Cliff explained. He noticed Mark hadn't said anything in response. "You said I should loosen the restraints."

"It probably is too soon." Mark had been afraid that Cliff had made the declaration lightly. It sounded so casual. "But I think I'm falling in love with you too." They stood there holding each other until the sizzling sound coming from the frying pan demanded Mark's attention.

Mark returned to the stove and dumped the still partially frozen mush into the frying pan. He covered the pan as Cliff came up from behind and put his arms around Mark's midsection. Within the confines of Cliff's arms, Mark turned around to kiss the man holding him. "The food will take a while. Why don't we go sit down?"

They spent the next half hour or so kissing and petting on the couch, broken only when Mark got up every once in a while to check the progress of their meal. Finally, Mark declared their dinner ready. "Could you give me a hand?"

The smell was wonderful, cinnamon and apple from the oven and another scent of roast chicken or something similar that Cliff couldn't quite place. He got up to join Mark, who was pulling plates from a cupboard above the sink. Cliff looked into the frying pan. It smelled good. The look was something else, a grayish mush toasted golden brown at the edges. "What's in this, exactly?" he asked tentatively.

"Potatoes and meat," Mark explained. It was tradition to serve it for holidays and special occasions along the South Shore. "Do you have any allergies?"

"No," Cliff answered, still observing the mush. "These Acadians could work on their presentation."

Mark laughed loudly. "Well, they were oppressed. I promise it tastes better than it looks." Giving the matter a little thought, he said, "It is an acquired taste. If you don't like it, we can get something else."

"It smells good," he said warily. Cliff was willing to try it.

Mark handed the plates to Cliff for him to hold. He then scooped a small helping of the mush into each.

"It's okay. You can give me more than that." Cliff was afraid he had been rude and offended his host.

"Trust me," Mark said lightly. "You probably won't need more."

Cliff placed the plates on the table. They sat. He watched as Mark put a pat of butter on the mush and followed his example by doing the same. He was surprised that there were no other vegetables or meat to go with the dish. He gave Mark a quizzical look as the other man poured molasses over the butter. "You're kidding?"

Mark grinned at the expression of disbelief on Cliff's face. "It's tradition but some people prefer just the butter."

Completely unsure about it, Cliff poured a few thick, dark ribbons over his steaming plate. Mark was watching him, still smirking. Resigned, Cliff picked up a fork and tried a bite. It was not what he'd expected. The texture was smooth. It tasted of roasted meat. Mark had been right, though. He wouldn't be able to eat a lot of it, but it was good.

"You are a brave man," Mark declared with a smile. He picked up his own fork and started eating.

When he finished his serving, Cliff was tempted to have just a little more.

THE LAST SNOW OF WINTER

As if reading his mind, Mark said, "There is more if you want it, but you might want to wait. It's a heavy meal when you're not used to it. Plus we have apple crisp for dessert."

Cliff considered it and took Mark's advice. "Do you want me to put that in a dish?" he said, indicating the leftovers in the frying pan.

"Please," Mark replied. He then added, "We should rinse out the pan too. It turns to cement if you let it sit."

"Good to know, since I just ate it." It felt so good to be doing this. Cliff hadn't experienced such a relaxed and comfortable evening with anyone outside of his own family. No, it was different from that. He was on guard with his family too.

After rinsing the plates and pan, they decided to wait a while for dessert. They moved to the living room to be more comfortable.

"Would you like music?" Mark asked.

"Whatever you want, Bobcat." He watched as Mark stepped into Jeff's room. Getting comfortable, Cliff spread his arms wide along the back of the couch. It was so good to be here. He took in the rather commonplace details of the room. Against the unremarkable backdrop, the shepherd painting stood out and caught his eye again.

Quiet music filtered unobtrusively into the air as Mark returned. His roommate had an impressive collection of music. Mark was afraid his own more limited selection might be a little too obscure for his guest. On entering the living room, Mark noticed Cliff looking so very at home. He paused to admire him.

"What?" Cliff asked when he became aware of Mark standing there watching.

"I just like looking at you," Mark confessed.

"Get over here, Bobcat." Cliff patted the couch beside him.

"So what do we do now?" Mark asked playfully as he sat down at the far end of the couch.

"I'd like you to tell me about yourself." Cliff reached over and pulled Mark closer.

Mark settled in next to the big man. He could feel the heat of his body. "What do you want to know?" As a subject of conversation, Mark was sure he wouldn't be that interesting.

"Where do those come from?" Cliff pointed to the painting on the wall.

The question wasn't what Mark had expected. While he was considering an answer, he realized it was a very shrewd question. For the most part, Mark was quite reserved, but painting allowed him to express himself. *What can I say?* "An artist friend once accused me of using art to expose my true self."

"Is it true?" Cliff looked again to the lion-shepherd.

"Yes, I suppose it is, in a way." The release wasn't one that Mark consciously planned, but over time it had developed on its own.

Cliff studied the look on Mark's face. "Could you show me more?"

Mark considered the request. "More of my artwork or more of myself?" He was flattered by the other man's interest but was determined that this wouldn't be completely one-sided. He knew so little about Cliff. "If I do, will you tell me more about yourself?"

"That seems fair enough," Cliff replied cautiously.

It was obvious that Cliff wasn't thrilled by the idea of reciprocating. "I promise I won't try to embarrass you. I just want to get to know you better. Why don't we have dessert first?" Mark suggested diplomatically.

The apple crisp was still warm. Mark only wished he had some whipped cream to serve with it. He was happy that Cliff seemed to enjoy the meal. They were sitting on either end of the couch again. Mark had recommended they eat in the living room. They weren't talking much as they ate. When Mark finished, he set his bowl on the coffee table and waited for Cliff. "Stay the night with me." Meant to be a question, it came out like an order.

Cliff set his plate next to Mark's. "Okay," he answered simply. He shifted on the couch and leaned back to put his head on the other man's lap. The wall with the painting was at his feet. With a self-satisfied smile for Mark, he asked with a nod toward the wall, "So are you the lion or the lamb?"

Gently caressing the smooth skin of Cliff's head, Mark admired his relaxed features and then followed the gaze of those striking blue eyes to the painting. "You're being too literal," he explained. "I'm not the subject." Mark paused long enough to arrange his thoughts. "The lion and the lamb have religious connotations, but that wasn't my intention. It just seemed to happen. I sometimes ask myself, is the shepherd a protector? Is the lamb for wool or food?" Mark contemplated the image while Cliff waited silently. "Look at the dog. It's a hunting dog, not a herding dog. I sometimes wonder what the lamb is thinking. Is it relieved to be rescued?"

"You created it. You talk about it like it was something you picked up somewhere." Cliff found the information both fascinating and bewildering.

Mark smiled at the assessment. "The process is organic. I start with an idea, an image in my head. Something I read, hear, or see triggers an idea. But it changes as I work." It was difficult for Mark to tell if this made sense to Cliff. "I'm usually disappointed with the result. That's how I can tell it's almost finished." He laughed at the confession. "After a few days or even weeks, the painting will begin to grow on me. I keep this one because I enjoy it. I give most of them away. I've done a few commissions, and a few have been sold."

"So what secret part of you is revealed here?" Cliff asked.

"Well." Mark considered the question. "Maybe some part of me feels lost and wants to be rescued." It felt strange to Mark to admit that aloud. "At other times I feel more like the shepherd. Maybe I want to do the rescuing."

Cliff looked into Mark's face. *Does this help me understand the man better? Perhaps it does.* He would have to give it more thought.

"Now, your turn," Mark informed Cliff, the corner of his mouth turning up in a ghost of a smile. He looked at the head resting in his lap and stroked the smooth scalp again. Hundreds of questions vied for attention. It was hard to settle on just one. Then a question seemed to come of itself. "Is this the real Cliff?"

"I'm not sure I understand what you want to know." A crease formed between Cliff's brows as he considered what Mark was asking.

"Out there," Mark said, cocking his head toward the door, "you come across as something between an outlaw biker and a professional wrestler. People practically cower when you look at them. The shaved head, the wild beard, the cold stare. I don't believe it." Mark was using his most soothing voice. Cliff sat up suddenly and moved away, making Mark wonder if he had assumed too much.

"This is what I look like." The tone was firm. Cliff wasn't aware of the turn of his features. He had retreated to his usual fierce front.

Mark was about to apologize but instinctively decided not to back down. "I'm not talking about your appearance. I'm asking about the character you play."

Cliff could now feel how he had tensed. The defenses were all up in full force. It took an effort, but he deliberately pushed them back down and took a few breaths to compose himself.

Watching the change and waiting silently, Mark wished he were as comfortable as he pretended to be. *Why can't you leave things alone? You always need to take stuff apart and see how it works.*

"You ask hard questions. No one has ever said something like that to me before," Cliff replied.

"I'm sorry." Mark felt it was time to apologize. "I just want to get to know you."

Cliff's expression softened a little. "I forgot that my gentle little bobcat is more dangerous than he appears. He asks questions that leave a person bleeding." The tension was lifting slowly. "I guess I do wear the tough guy image as body armor. I've done it for so long, it feels normal to me." Cliff stopped to consider the idea.

It felt too soon for Mark to ask more from him. He didn't want to really upset the guy.

Noticing the other man's stillness, Cliff observed, "Even when you don't say anything, I can feel a compulsion to respond to what I know you want." He joked, "You have control over me that I never expected. Be gentle."

Relaxed again and feeling himself to be on better footing, Mark teased, "Y'big moose."

Cliff pulled the smaller man into a hug to chase off the last of the tension. He let his reservations go and opened up completely. He spoke quietly. "My older brother was killed in an accident when I was still quite young. Ryan was an all-around super-masculine guy. He was into girls, sports, cars, and everything. I guess I felt pressure to live up to him. You know, carry on the family name and all that." While it felt good to let this out, it was still harder than Cliff had expected. He had to push himself to keep going. "Ryan and I used to toss around the football. He played in high school. I wanted to be just like him. Then there was the accident. Mom hated that he drove a motorcycle." Cliff trailed off, apparently lost in his own thoughts.

Mark felt the need to do something, say something. Cliff looked up at him and seemed to read his feelings from his expression.

"It's enough that you're here." Cliff took a restoring breath. "I knew early on I was gay. I kept it hidden. I did everything I could to live up to my brother's memory. My parents are proud, but they don't really know me." Cliff was afraid he was beginning to ramble.

"I know what that's like," Mark said thoughtfully.

Cliff nodded. "It feels good to be with you. I can let go and be myself, but I don't know that person as well as the tough guy. You have to be patient and give me time."

"That sounds fair." The request for patience pleased Mark. It sounded like the big guy was planning on staying around. They chatted comfortably after that, talking about little things, likes and dislikes and stories from their childhoods. Cliff had put his head back in Mark's lap. It made him happy that Cliff seemed so comfortable with him.

After stifling a few yawns and noticing that Cliff was doing the same, Mark said, "Why don't we go to bed?" It was as if the tension from earlier had drained them both.

Cliff yawned in agreement. "Okay."

Mark's bed was a double. It was perfectly adequate for him alone, though his toes did stick out past the end of the mattress when he stretched out. It would be a bit tight for the two of them. *Well, it'll be cozy*, he reasoned.

Without waiting for Mark to ask, Cliff helped him off with his clothes. The smooth, warm skin he exposed begged for the touch of Cliff's hands. He caught sight of the two of them in the mirror above a low dresser. Even in the dim light, the difference between them was dramatic. The warm color and long, graceful lines of the one contrasted with the pale, cream skin and substantial bulk of the other. Mark looked so small in his arms. There was no point in trying to hide his excitement; Cliff's cock had a mind of its own.

The quilt on Mark's bed was a gift from his grand-mère. *I'm sure this wasn't what she had in mind when she gave it to me*, Mark thought wryly. Pulling the quilt back, he exposed the sheets underneath. Unexpectedly, he felt himself pushed down onto the bed. Mark twisted around in time to watch as Cliff crawled onto him, holding him down with his body.

"I want you." Cliff's voice was gravel.

"You have me," Mark said simply in reply.

Cliff absorbed the look Mark gave him. The look conveyed trust. Cliff shivered in the power of it. Leaning closer, he kissed his lover. Part of Cliff's consciousness reminded him of his responsibilities. In response, he lifted off his lover and swiftly left the room. A moment later, Mark heard a thump and a faint curse from the darkened living room. It took him a second to realize what Cliff was doing. The overhead light clicked on in the living room, followed by an inarticulate sound of satisfaction. The light clicked off, and Cliff was standing in the doorway again.

"I thought you had changed your mind," Mark said, relieved that it wasn't so.

Holding the condom box and the bottle of lube, Cliff answered, "Not a chance." He tossed the bottle onto the bed next to Mark and began fighting with one of the foil packets. "Shit!" Eventually, he got it open.

Mark had to respect the other man's single-minded determination. He was smiling as he watched the man struggle. When Cliff caught the expression, Mark joked, "Oh oh, I seem to have provoked the beast."

Cliff climbed onto the bed, lifting and spreading Mark's legs to expose his ass. "Is this what you want, Bobcat?" Cliff pressed his cock against the opening.

"Yes." The sound was barely more than a hiss. Mark wanted it very much.

Thankful that the lube bottle cooperated, Cliff slicked himself as well as the area around Mark's hole. It was impossible to wait any longer. He began pushing at the opening with his thick, blunt cock. He could feel it giving way. Mark's sharp gasp cooled him a little. He slowed his assault, but hot flesh gradually allowed him entry and then held him tight. He was deep inside Mark now.

His body was protesting, but Mark didn't care. Cliff's passion fueled his own. Once accommodated, Cliff's cock felt impossibly huge inside him. The sensation of fullness was overwhelming, but Mark couldn't get enough. Cliff was moving in and out now. Mark wrapped his legs around his lover's body instinctively to pull him even closer.

Cliff was surprised when he felt Mark wrap strong legs around him. Losing balance, he fell forward. He threw his arms out to either side of Mark to brace himself. His face hung over Mark's face, their hot breath mingling. Their chests were almost touching. Cliff was pleased to discover he could fuck his lover and kiss him at the same time. They kissed hungrily. It was too much. Cliff snapped his head back and yelled with the climax.

Mark felt the spasm of Cliff's cock inside his body. After the initial climax, the big man sagged onto him. His arm was uncomfortably pinned between them, and he would need to move it soon, but he was temporarily content to stay just as they were. As if understanding the unspoken need, Cliff lifted himself off Mark's body and pulled out slowly. Mark uncurled, letting his legs drop to the mattress. He could see Cliff standing at the foot of the bed, breathing hard, his skin flushed red under russet fur. He lusted after the big bear.

Rolling to bring his feet to the floor, Mark deliberately made his way to the giant. Cliff was still standing at the foot of the bed as if in a trance, watching. Placing a hand on the bigger man's cheek, Mark drew him into a tender kiss. "I'm wondering how adventurous you are," Mark whispered.

Cliff knew what he was asking. He had never done that before. In his mind, there was a certain stigma to letting a man mount him and take him. *But it's Mark.*

"You don't have to," Mark said gently.

The words shook him. Mark wouldn't take him, but he could give himself to Mark. That made all the difference. "I want to. I've just never done that before."

"We can try if you like, but only if you're sure." Mark remembered his first time. They had both been inexperienced, and it had hurt like hell. "I'll go slowly, and we can stop anytime."

Cliff let Mark guide him to lie back on the bed. This was something he wanted to do. He needed to do it. His bobcat would take care of him.

Mark took his time, making sure Cliff was relaxed. The excitement he felt was tempered by the trust he was being given. Using an ample amount of lubricant, Mark began gently massaging Cliff's furry hole. He kept up a stream of gently soothing words, telling Cliff what was happening, what to expect, and what to do. "Relax. Trust me. I won't hurt you."

Senses heightened by the recent climax and the intensity of the situation, Cliff nearly yelled when Mark slipped a finger smoothly into his opening. Instead of a yell, it came out as a gasp. The sensation was novel and difficult to describe. Mark was patient, taking his time, nothing like how he had just barged in. The thought caused him a pang of guilt. Unexpectedly, Cliff heard himself groaning. Something bigger was pushing its way into his body. The sensation was dominating his consciousness. He was awash in it. In and out, gently stretching the opening all the time. Cliff was lost in the moment.

Time passed. A shift of weight on the bed alerted him that something was going to change. Cliff felt Mark lifting his legs, one at a time. Then there was a welcome touch against his most private place. The pressure built gently. He didn't fight it. *Mark told me to relax, and Mark is always right.* The idea made him smile inside. *Inside! He's inside me.* Cliff could feel it. Mark wasn't moving, but he was inside.

It took a considerable effort for Mark to hold back. He had loosened Cliff's tight hole and was now just inside. His teddy bear was watching him, trust on his face. Mark pulled back slowly, not all the way out, just enough. He pushed back in a little deeper this time. After waiting to give Cliff time to adjust, he repeated the action. It had been a long time since Mark had last done this. He knew he wasn't going to be able to hold himself back for long.

Cliff groaned in pleasure. He'd had no idea. It felt so full. He could feel his cock responding to the sensations, filling with blood, heavy on his stomach. His hand found his cock and stroked it. The rhythm was getting faster. Mark was almost pounding his ass. Cliff felt the other man's balls press against his stretched hole, his cock buried deep. It was too much.

Mark didn't make much noise when he came, but, he reflected with humor, Cliff more than made up for that. He pulled out slowly and crawled up next to his lover, who was still shivering with his second climax of the night. "So what do you think, Teddy Bear?"

"I think my brain has turned to liquid and is running out my ears," Cliff said. His eyes were unfocused.

Still a little shaky, Mark was content to rest a few minutes and recover before cleaning up. Eyes closed, Cliff lay beside him. The pattern of Cliff's breathing was becoming deeper and more regular. Not wanting to fall asleep himself, Mark padded off to the bathroom to get a cloth to clean up his lover.

Once they were both clean, Mark threw the quilt over Cliff and joined him under the covers. His lover's large frame was warm and comforting. As he suspected, Cliff took up too much of the bed. It might be a problem in the future, but for tonight, Mark was happy to curl up securely next to him. Unlike the last two nights, Mark quickly drifted off to sleep, lulled by rhythmical breathing that was almost a snore.

Chapter 15

LIGHT filled the room. *Something is definitely wrong. The light is on the wrong side of the bed. The window should be on the other side of the room.* Cliff formed these thoughts with a perfectly unreasonable frustration in a universe that somehow had it wrong today. *Otherwise, I'm sleeping the wrong way, which is ridiculous.* It took a few more moments for Cliff to remember he wasn't at home. He turned and nearly rolled over Mark, who, up to now, had been sleeping peacefully.

"Morning, Moose," Mark grumbled sleepily in response to the unceremonious wakeup call.

"Your bed's too small," informed Cliff. "So, do you still respect me?"

"Who said I respected you yesterday?" The retort came quickly. Mark usually woke alert. Too late, he saw the look of sadistic amusement form on Cliff's face. *Oops, that was probably a mistake,* he realized too late.

Cliff pinned and tickled the smaller man until Mark begged for mercy.

"Stop. Stop! I still respect you." Mark was painfully aware of how physically outmatched he was in this partnership. Still, he trusted the man. Nearly breathless, he begged, "I'll do whatever you want."

Letting up the tickle torture, Cliff answered, "I'll hold you to that." He took a kiss as down payment and slipped off the bed to visit the bathroom.

Mark watched him go. The strange dichotomy between the playful lover and the unapproachable tough guy had him uncertain. He turned his eyes away from the empty doorway to break the trance he had fallen into. Noticing his bag on the desk, Mark considered the work he still had to do. He hadn't accomplished any schoolwork yesterday. Laundry and tidying up had eaten up the entire afternoon, and he was supposed to be catching the train today. *Should I change my plans?*

A shadow loomed in the doorway, and the movement attracted Mark's eye. He took in the stocky, muscled form with pleasure as Cliff stood there naked, returning the scrutiny boldly. Mark found it hard to imagine what the big guy saw in him. They were so different.

"I would offer to make you breakfast, but this is your place," Cliff said.

Mark was mildly envious that Cliff seemed completely unselfconscious about his body. "Is that a hint that I'm falling down in my duties as host?" Lifting off the bed as he spoke, Mark reached for the robe he usually wore in the morning. Fingers touched the fabric, but he didn't put it on. He wondered what he could give Cliff to wear. It would hardly be fair to let his guest go naked.

"I didn't want to complain." Cliff smiled playfully.

"Time to feed the bear again," Mark said with a dramatic sigh. Walking up to Cliff, he explained, "I've got nothing here that will fit you, except maybe a blanket. Not that I don't like the view." They were standing close now. "But I don't want you to get cold."

Putting his arms around Mark, Cliff said thoughtfully, "Good morning, Bobcat." They kissed sweetly, bumping noses unintentionally, which made them laugh. Cliff held his lover tightly. The heat from Mark's bed-warmed body felt inviting in the chilly air. "I'll take that blanket."

Mark reached for his robe and then pulled a throw blanket out of the closet and handed it over. Leading the way to the kitchen, he warned, "I don't know what I have to eat. I'm running low on food."

THE LAST SNOW OF WINTER

With a little digging and more than a little luck, they managed to prepare a breakfast of pancakes made from an instant mix that Mark had completely forgotten about. The morning passed by pleasantly in a picture of domestic simplicity. At one point, Mark stopped what he was doing just to watch Cliff moving comfortably about the kitchen in his underwear with the blanket draped over his wide shoulders and tied loosely at his neck like a superhero's cape. The sight brought a smile to Mark's face. There was something familiar in the image. It skirted the edge of his consciousness. Slipping deeper into thought, Mark's features relaxed, and his eyes became unfocused. *It reminds me of something.* It took a few seconds for him to make the connection. *I'm thinking of the shepherd in the painting.* He shivered involuntarily at the realization but then shook off the feeling.

Dishes washed, they showered and cleaned up for the day. Separate showers this time. The shower in the cottage was too small for the two of them to use together. It was almost too small for Cliff's large frame alone. Mark listened with amusement to the occasional muffled sounds of protest coming from the bathroom while he waited his turn.

After his own shower, Mark studied his face in the mirror above the sink. He hadn't shaved since Friday and decided his neck and cheeks were looking a bit scruffy. Mark disliked shaving as a rule and wore a short beard as a way of minimizing the unwelcome task. On the other hand, he was conscientious about keeping it tidy. Could he manage the job on his own? Mark wasn't convinced he could. He was still lost in thought, staring into the mirror, when Cliff found him.

"Are you okay?" Cliff asked with a little concern on seeing the faraway look in Mark's eyes.

Coming around quickly, Mark replied, "Oh, I'm fine. I was just wondering if I could manage shaving myself."

Standing behind Mark and addressing the face in the mirror, Cliff said quietly, "You could let me help you."

An entire conversation ran swiftly through Mark's mind. First, he would politely decline the offered assistance. Then, offended by the refusal, Cliff would insist on helping, claiming his right as friend. Each step of the imaginary argument, clearly laid out for his mind's eye. Instead of replying, Mark said nothing and looked to the face reflected beside his own in the mirror. He could read the same thoughts there. He smiled in response to the realization.

Rather than acknowledging the unspoken exchange, Cliff simply returned the smile and said, "Why don't we get started?"

"Okay."

Like many of his colleagues studying in the field of life sciences, Mark had a certain degree of pro-environmental leanings. His resistance to driving and insistence on walking whenever possible was just one example. He also chose to use a shaving mug and brush rather than buy shaving cream in an aerosol can. The anachronism was an interesting novelty for Cliff. He had seen a shaving mug before but had never used one. With a little instruction, he successfully lathered up the brush and applied the foam at first playfully and then with more care to Mark's face. Bare-chested, Cliff in his underwear and Mark in a towel, the two men stood close together in front of the sink.

"Are you ready?" Cliff asked. Mark only nodded.

Cliff gestured to Mark, indicating he should raise his head. In a long, steady stroke of the razor, Cliff removed a line of the thin foam from Mark's skin. Intent on the task, Cliff rinsed the blade and repeated the action.

At first amused by the procedure, Cliff's intensity soon mesmerized Mark. The strength and power contained in the man standing before him was irresistible. The physical strength was obvious to everyone, but Mark hadn't suspected the level of mental discipline that went with it. In the face of it, Mark became suddenly shy.

The whole procedure of shaving only took a few minutes. Cliff wiped away the last of the residue with a wet facecloth. He kissed Mark and looked into his eyes questioningly. "Did I do okay?" he asked.

Mark shook his head and then, feeling stupid for not speaking, said, "Yeah... thank you."

"I'm going to go get ready." Cliff looked again into Mark's eyes and smiled before leaving the room.

Dressing by himself in the bedroom, Cliff spared a few minutes to inspect the painting above the bed. He had been too preoccupied to give it much attention earlier. He studied it now. The painting was a realistic representation of a wide, flat landscape with distant mountains on the horizon, all under the cover of a big sky. A chain-link fence ran the full width of the canvas, separating the viewer from a small airport runway. The fence dominated the foreground. Leaning against it was a man, who stood back-to, watching two small planes that might be landing or taking off. *What does this tell you about Mark?* Cliff couldn't say.

When Cliff emerged from the bedroom dressed in the clothes he'd worn the afternoon before, Mark came face to face with the precarious nature of their situation. *Now what?* He didn't want to pressure the man or come across as too needy, but he wanted to know that he could see him again soon.

"I have a meeting today before lunch," Cliff said absently as he tucked in his shirt. His mind was still considering possible messages hidden in the painting above the bed. The expression on Mark's face pulled his attention to the present. "What's wrong?" When Mark didn't answer, Cliff said, "Aww, is my little bobcat going to miss me?"

Close to the truth, Mark tried to make a joke of it. "No. Why would I miss you? You big moose."

"Come on. What's up?" Cliff insisted, crossing his arms. "If we are going to do this, we need to be honest with each other."

Mark knew he was right. "I didn't expect dating to be easy. I guess I had no idea how insecure I was going to be."

"It's hard for me too," Cliff admitted. "What's got you brooding today?"

"I'm supposed to be catching the train this afternoon," Mark admitted.

"Oh." It was Cliff's turn to feel undone. He made an effort to shake it off. They hadn't made any plans after all. *What's it to you if Mark is going away for the week?*

Mark caught the quick flash of emotion. In private, he seemed to be able to read Cliff very well. It was only when the big guy retreated to his public face that Mark found him inscrutable. Although he was covering it up, it was obvious that Cliff was disappointed. "Aww, is my big teddy bear going to miss me?"

"I don't know what you're talking about." Caught, Cliff felt a little foolish. *Nothing for it*, he realized. *Time to come clean.* "I guess I thought we'd have more time alone together, just the two of us. You know, without all the distractions of real life." It seemed perfect in his head. "You and I together for March break." Cliff could suddenly appreciate that it was a big assumption on his part.

"It could still be that way." It took almost no time for Mark to decide. "I can always change my plans."

"I can't ask you to do that," Cliff said.

"You don't have to ask me." Mark felt strangely buoyant in the discovery that Cliff was just as smitten as he was. "I have stuff to do, and I won't be able to do it at my parents' place." He presented the point in a matter-of-fact tone. "Besides...." Mark's voice softened as he said, "If I left now, I wouldn't be fit to be around."

"And why is that?" Cliff asked automatically.

"Because I'd be missing you the whole time, you big moose," Mark admitted.

"What about your family?" Cliff wasn't particularly close to his own family but didn't want to keep Mark from his.

"I'll be seeing them in a few weeks anyway." While Mark had been looking forward to seeing his friends and family, he knew he would be miserable if he went. Being with Cliff was the only thing on his mind right now.

Cliff considered what Mark was offering. "This may sound selfish, but I'd like it if you stayed." He had to admit, he had been extremely unhappy at the possibility of losing Mark. It was ridiculous, he knew. Mark would come back soon enough. He looked at his watch. "I want to talk about this, but I really need to get going."

"If you give me a few minutes, I can walk with you." Mark waited until Cliff nodded his head in the affirmative. "I just have to get dressed and grab a few things."

The sky was overcast but not especially dark. From experience, Mark expected that the gray would clear soon enough. The deep freeze of winter was starting to let go. Spring was still to come, but winter was losing its icy hold. "Can we talk as we walk, or did you want to wait 'til later?" He was curious about what it was that Cliff wanted to discuss.

It puzzled Cliff that while he trusted Mark in the most intimate physical way possible, he still found it hard to say what he wanted to say. *You let him fuck you. You told him you love him. Open your damn mouth and talk.* Suitably chastised, he said, "It seems to me that we've jumped ahead to the middle of this story when we should be still in the introduction."

"You're probably right." It was too fast, but Mark didn't want to stop. Was that what Cliff wanted?

"I'm not saying I'm sorry." *What am I trying to say?* Cliff paused to rearrange his thoughts. "I guess I'm a little unsure where we stand."

"Me too," Mark admitted freely. Hints of blue in the gray overhead indicated where the sun was threatening to break through the cloud cover. Mark watched, but the sun remained hidden.

They were about halfway between the cottage and town. Cliff still hadn't said what he wanted to say. He still wasn't completely sure what he wanted to say. "I have a proposition to make."

Arching his eyebrows, Mark turned to Cliff but didn't say anything.

"I don't mean like that, you little hussy." Cliff felt his mood lighten. It would be okay, he realized. "We have a week to get to know each other better. We practically have the town to ourselves. What I'm proposing is that for this one week, we let go. No fears. No reservations. You and I are together."

Mark had been about to joke that he didn't have anything left to proposition after the last two days. The offer Cliff was making pushed the joke completely out of his head. Instead, he asked, "So for a week we would be... boyfriends?"

"Boyfriends, lovers, a couple, whatever. It's crazy. It's too fast, but I don't care. I want to be with you." Breathing fast without noticing, Cliff waited impatiently to hear what Mark would say.

"Wow." It was easy for Mark to admit he wanted this.

"It's probably a mistake," Cliff cautioned.

The observation echoed Mark's thoughts precisely, but he knew he was going to say yes. "You're right. It probably is a mistake. But I want to."

Forgetting where they were, Cliff grabbed Mark about the middle and swung him around. Mark's grunt, rather than propriety, persuaded Cliff to put him back down.

"Is this what I'm going to have to put up with?" Mark flexed the fingers of his right hand. It wasn't that bad. Cliff had just caught him by surprise.

"Yes, but you already agreed. It's too late to change your mind now." Cliff walked on, the picture of sobriety. Only the smile in his eyes told of the happiness he was feeling.

"Just for clarity's sake," Mark asked, "I take it public displays are off limits?"

Cliff sobered even more. He looked to Mark a little sheepishly and said, "You're right. I still need to be careful."

"Agreed! No jumping each other in public places." It amused Mark that Cliff was the one having trouble keeping himself under control.

THE LAST SNOW OF WINTER

The two men walked on silently. Each lost in their own thoughts. Mark was almost startled when Cliff exclaimed abruptly, "I keep expecting you to bolt!"

Surprised by the statement, Mark asked, "What do you mean?"

"You could have any guy," Cliff said. "Why do you want to put up with me?"

The confusion Mark experienced on hearing the question was clear in his voice as he asked, "Where is this coming from?" He waited, but Cliff didn't say anything. "Look, Teddy Bear. You, sir, are a catch. You're smart—" Cliff was about to protest, but Mark held up a hand, shook his head, and continued. "Sexy, funny, and hot as hell. I'm the one who should feel outclassed."

Cliff thought about that. Could he accept what Mark was saying? Mark felt so precious to him. "We're a good pair, I guess."

Shaking his head again but smiling this time, Mark said gently, "You big moose."

That made Cliff smile too. He was "Teddy Bear" when Mark was feeling tender, and he was "a big moose" when Mark was frustrated with him. Just like that, nice and simple. Cliff liked it. They reached the corner of the street where Cliff lived. Checking his watch, he saw there wasn't time to go home and change. He would have to meet his mentor dressed as he was.

They walked past Cliff's street and continued on to the campus. The sky overhead was open now with wispy clouds framing a vault of clear blue. Mark hadn't observed the change. The sunshine suited his mood. He bobbed his head to music only he could hear. Mark noticed Cliff glance toward him and smile without making a comment.

As they approached the lower doors of the B.A.C., Cliff said, "I don't know how long I'll be. I don't think I can meet you for lunch."

"That's okay. I have a lot to do." He didn't want the big guy to think he was that insecure. It was then that another possibility occurred to Mark. Maybe that wasn't the point at all. "Could we meet later for supper?"

"I'd like that." Cliff brightened at once. "Why don't you come by my place? Around five? You can help me throw something together." Definite plans reassured Cliff. Now that he was sure to see Mark later, he felt he could concentrate on what he should be doing today. "I'll see you later." He turned to go but paused midway. "Damn. I want to kiss you." The words came out quietly even though there was no one else around to hear them.

"I know." Mark could feel it too. "You will later."

They were just inside the building now. Cliff turned and strode away with deliberation. Watching until the other man disappeared from sight up the stairs, Mark made an effort to stir himself. He had things to do and plans for later. The fact filled him with pleasure.

Coming back to the present, Mark noticed bright light flooding the art gallery. The general lights were on at their full intensity, which was as unusual as the total darkness had been two nights before. During shows, individual spots on the artwork provided the only illumination. The general lights were rarely ever on. As he walked by, Mark could see several packing crates arranged seemingly haphazardly around the interior of the gallery. Standing amidst the chaos was Dawn.

On seeing Dawn, Mark instantly experienced a surge of guilt. He and Dawn had been friends for years. They had been very close as friends. What Mark hadn't realized was that Dawn wanted to take things even further. It was less than six months ago that Mark had first understood that Dawn had a crush on him. He had missed all the signs for ages. When the one-sided attraction became obvious even to Mark, he tried to ignore it. Surely, Dawn would come to her senses, he had thought. Eventually Mark knew he had to do something to set things right.

Uncomfortable in a lie, Mark told the truth. He came out to Dawn. It went well enough, considering. No, that wasn't true. She took the news well enough, but it strained their friendship possibly to the breaking point. Dawn was suddenly very busy all the time. They had barely spoken in the last three or four weeks.

THE LAST SNOW OF WINTER

As fate would have it, Dawn saw him walking by through the glass. Mark offered her a friendly wave. To his surprise, she got up and walked to the door of the gallery. Mark changed course, veering toward the door and wondering at the change in behavior.

"Hi," Dawn said casually once she had unlocked and opened the door. "I'm surprised to see you. I thought you would be visiting your family." Blonde hair tied back, she was wearing comfortable clothes suited to the task of unpacking the boxes spread around the room. "It's been quite a while since we've talked."

Mark didn't know how to respond. He certainly wasn't going to comment on the reason behind the estrangement. Instead, he said, "It's good to see you." Uncertain about what to say next, he inquired about the show. "What are you putting up today?"

Dawn was an art history student and worked part-time in the gallery. She motioned Mark in so they could talk while she worked. "It's a fiber show," she said. "It features weaving of many sorts. There are several pieces I'm sure you'll like." She pointed out a large wooden crate that was open on one side, indicating Mark should look inside. Suspended in the crate was a branch with the color and sheen of copper. The leaves were obviously woven metal but looked like gossamer. Even partially hidden by the protective packing material, it was a stunning sight.

"Beautiful!" Dawn was right. It was exactly suited to Mark's tastes. Feeling guilty again at the hopefully temporary break in their friendship, Mark wondered what he should have done differently.

"I'm the first one here. I was just checking that everything arrived safely." Dawn picked up a bright red clipboard from the corner of a nearby crate. "What happened to your arm?" she asked, noticing the sling for the first time.

Mark had forgotten his injury. "Oh, I fell. It isn't serious."

Accepting that, Dawn said, "The show opens tonight." She turned back to the box she had been unpacking. "Everything arrived late. It will be tight, but the opening starts at seven." She waited a few seconds before adding, "You should come."

"I'd like that." It felt like the first thaw of ice on a river in spring, slow and ponderous. Mark hoped the thaw would continue, and they could go back to being friends. "I'll let you get back to work."

"Do you think you'll come?" Dawn questioned tentatively.

"I'll try." The answer sounded terrible in his ears, but Mark already had plans with Cliff. He didn't want to commit and then disappoint her. He and Dawn had made it a tradition to go to every opening they could together. Missing this tonight would make the break in their friendship especially real. Mark said his goodbye and headed for the computer lab, feeling less happy than he had been.

Chapter 16

Professor Hansen's office was cheerfully sunny. Lined with books and filled to overflowing with papers, the small room appeared even smaller. Cliff knocked on the doorframe to announce himself. The door was open as usual. The man working at the desk by the window looked up at the sound and smiled in recognition and welcome.

"Perfect timing," he said warmly. Dr. Hansen removed his glasses and placed them on the papers he had been reading. While he was in his fifties, his hair was still smooth and dark with barely a trace of gray. He motioned Cliff to one of the chairs positioned around a circular worktable. Noticing how his guest was dressed, he observed, "You're looking good today. Special occasion?"

It took a moment for Cliff to grasp the meaning behind the question. Remembering, he glanced down at his clothing self-consciously and replied, "I had a date last night, and I was a bit rushed this morning." Dr. Hansen was a mentor for Cliff's honors thesis. He was encouraging Cliff to work toward his Masters degree and perhaps even more. Over the last few years, they had also become good friends.

"Well, I hope the young lady treated you well," Dr. Hansen commented good-naturedly as he took his usual chair at the table.

Cliff considered how he should reply. "I was well-treated, Professor." The half-truth made him feel dishonest. It was like lying to his father.

Catching some of the conflict, the professor apologized. "Hmmm, none of my business. Sorry for the intrusion." Then, businesslike again, "Should we get to work?"

Lost in his own thoughts, Cliff didn't respond. He was still standing by the table with his hand on the back of a chair. He didn't notice the perceptive look the other man was giving him. The pause in conversation finally woke him, and he muttered "Sorry" before taking a seat.

"Do you want to talk about it?" Dr. Hansen asked.

Cliff couldn't help the little smile. *Psychologists. You can't get anything past them. Why not take advantage of the offer?* Tentatively, Cliff said, "Ted, we've known each other for a while."

"Yes," he agreed. The use of the familiar name indicated this was a personal matter and not school-related. They indeed knew each other well enough for Cliff to use his given name. Dr. Hansen rose and discreetly closed the door to his office before returning to his chair.

"I had a date last night... with another man," Cliff explained.

"Oh." Ted considered the disclosure for a few seconds. "That is a bit of a surprise, but I think you know me well enough to know that it isn't a big deal to me. This isn't the Dark Ages anymore."

"I know, but it's a big deal for me." This was the first friend he had come out to, Cliff realized. More than that, Dr. Hansen was like a father to him. The experience was both terrifying and liberating.

"It's a big deal to tell me, or it's a big deal that you had a date with a man?" Dr. Hansen wondered aloud. He leaned back into his chair to listen.

"Both. I've not done either before." A strange sense of excitement bordering on joy was spreading through Cliff. He'd told someone, and his world hadn't come to an end.

"I'm glad you felt you could tell me." As a practicing psychologist, Dr. Hansen could appreciate how difficult this must be for Cliff. He pushed aside the papers they had met to discuss. "Why don't you tell me more?"

Cliff knew better than to disagree. He could also recognize that it would be good for him to open up to his friend and mentor. He settled back in his chair and recapped the events of the last few days.

Dr. Hansen listened quietly, interrupting only occasionally to ask a leading question or to clarify a point. The confession had certainly been a surprise. He admonished himself for his own prejudices. The man sitting across from him may be a football player, but he was also a talented and dedicated student. There was no reason he couldn't also be gay. Still, he had to admit he wouldn't have put money on it.

Almost three hours passed. Cliff was shocked when he noticed. "I am so sorry. I've wasted your time."

"Not at all," Dr. Hansen responded, waving the apology off. "I'm glad I could be here to listen. I do have to go, and we'll have to reschedule our meeting, but I consider this as time well spent." He patted Cliff's broad shoulder in a familiar, fatherly way. "Why don't you come for dinner tomorrow night? Bring your friend with you. I'd like to meet him."

"I… I don't know." The prospect of a night out as a couple was daunting. "I could ask."

"You do that." Dr. Hansen collected up his papers and tossed them into a battered briefcase. "I'll talk to Carla, but I don't think it will be a problem. I'm looking forward to meeting this young man who has stolen your heart."

Cliff blushed at the words.

Observing the reaction to his comment, Dr. Hansen said, "Hmmm. This has been an interesting day. See you tomorrow at, say… six? Good." He ushered Cliff out the door and followed, closing the office door behind them.

Walking alone across campus, Cliff considered stopping at the computer lab to see if Mark was still there. He was feeling exhilarated after the encounter with his mentor. *No,* he told himself, *you'll see him soon enough. Let him work.* He had to reinforce his resolve as he neared the B.A.C. Deciding not to tempt himself, he walked around the block rather than taking the shorter route through the building itself.

He would need to pick up some groceries if he was going to supply dinner tonight. Thirty minutes later, Cliff stood looking blankly at the meat counter in the grocery store. *What am I going to make for supper?* He never gave meals much thought. His repertoire was limited. Settling on cold cuts for sandwiches, he quickly collected what he needed and pushed the cart to the checkout.

THE lighting in the computer lab was always relatively subdued. The room was essentially underground, so the lighting was completely artificial. Mark suspected the low light levels were deliberate, to help counter the problem of cooling the closed space. What with all the sensitive electronics dumping heat into the room, temperature control was a challenge. The unchanging lighting made it difficult to judge the passage of time. Looking around, Mark was surprised to see the clock on the wall indicating it was shortly past 4:00. Time to get going, he told himself. There would be plenty of time to get to Cliff's place, but he wanted to make a stop on the way.

Mark bounded up the stairs to Cliff's apartment carrying the parcel he'd picked up from a shop downtown. He could feel the butterflies fluttering around his insides again. *Surely, this will get easier*, he thought. He took a steadying breath before knocking a little tentatively on the door. He was about to knock again when the door opened. Seeing Cliff, Mark felt his apprehension lift. He knew he must be grinning like a fool, but he didn't care.

Cliff pulled Mark inside, closed the door, and kissed him hungrily. "I missed you," he exclaimed between kisses.

"I missed you too," Mark admitted. "I brought you something."

"Besides yourself?" Cliff asked. He watched in surprise as Mark presented him with a wedge-shaped paper package that obviously contained flowers. "You bugger." Cliff could feel a lump forming in his throat. "You're going to make me cry." The complaint was only half in jest.

Mark laughed. "I think you'll live."

Cliff unfolded a tab of paper to reveal the contents. Inside was a bundle of flawless red tulips, the delicate buds just beginning to open. Unable to speak, Cliff brought the flowers to his nose. His emotions were running unchecked. He pulled Mark into a tight, one-armed hug. "Thank you," he said hoarsely. They exchanged a sweet kiss.

The reaction to the gift was more than Mark had expected. He was pleased. "You're welcome, Teddy Bear." He watched as Cliff moved to the kitchen, mumbling something about a vase. "The woman at the florist shop said they were the perfect choice for a declaration of love. She seemed quite tickled that I was buying flowers for a special someone. I don't think she was picturing the same thing I was."

When Cliff returned with the flowers in a tall beer glass, he seemed more himself. "You didn't have to do this."

"I wanted to," Mark admitted. "Besides, I wouldn't have missed that reaction for the world."

"I've had a pretty emotional day," Cliff confessed.

"Oh, anything you can share?" Mark asked.

"I came out to the professor who is mentoring me for my honors thesis." The incident still seemed a little unreal to Cliff.

"Wow!" Mark said with surprise. *That was a big step.* "How did it go?"

"Great!" Cliff still felt overjoyed by the experience. He was happy to have Mark there to share it with and was conscious of the fact that it was largely thanks to Mark that it had happened in the first place.

The two men sat together on the couch as Cliff spent the next twenty minutes explaining what had happened. He didn't tell Mark everything he and Dr. Hansen had shared in their conversation, just the highlights. The process had brought Cliff closer to his friend and mentor. He suspected the distance that had been there was his own doing. Keeping quiet about his sexuality had placed an imperceptible divide between them. He hadn't even realized it was there.

"Dr. Hansen sounds like a pretty decent guy," Mark observed when Cliff finished. He wished he'd had someone like that to talk with when he was first dealing with his sexuality as a teen. Instead, Mark had spent the time taking long, lonely walks along the bluffs near his parents' home. In time, he learned to cope, but it had been a difficult period.

"He is," Cliff admitted. "You'll get to meet him tomorrow." He hoped that Mark would be okay with that. It seemed important somehow. Cliff was anxious to introduce Mark to a person whose opinion he greatly respected.

"Oh?"

"He invited us to dinner," Cliff explained. He hoped Mark would say yes.

"Us?" Mark asked. *Well, that's an interesting turn.*

"Will you go?" Cliff was anxious for Mark's answer.

"Yes, of course."

"Good." Relieved, Cliff rose to make something for them to eat.

"Hey, Teddy Bear, would you be interested in attending an opening this evening?" Mark figured this was a good time to ask, considering they were going out to dinner tomorrow as a couple.

Cliff stopped in his tracks halfway to the kitchen and turned to face Mark. "An opening?"

"The art gallery is opening a new show this evening," Mark explained. "I usually attend the openings, if I can."

Cliff considered the idea. "I would be your date?"

"You could go as my friend. But technically, yes, I suppose you would be my date." Mark wasn't sure where Cliff was going with this line of reasoning. He watched him standing there, apparently deep in thought.

After taking some time to mull it over, Cliff answered by saying simply, "I'd like to go."

"Good." Mark leaned back into the couch to get comfortable. "Care to tell me what was going on behind the scenes?"

A little surprised by the question, Cliff shrugged and said, "Well, I've never been to anything like that. It should be interesting. I think it would be fun to see this world you belong to." Cliff noticed that Mark was listening to him in that same quiet, patient way he always did. Mark always treated him like an intelligent being and seemed to want to hear what he had to say. "I was considering the prospect of being out in public together. And I was also a little worried that I might embarrass you in front of your friends."

Wrinkling his brow at hearing this admission, Mark said a little too sharply, "What? Why would you think that?"

"I don't know anything about art," Cliff offered lamely, shifting his weight from foot to foot uncomfortably.

"Well, that's...." Mark was at a loss. "I don't care if you don't know about art. Do I embarrass you because I don't know anything about football?"

"You could never embarrass me." Cliff could tell Mark was seriously irritated. *What did I do wrong?*

Mark made an effort to calm himself. "Look, you and I don't have to share the same interests to be friends. We are unique individuals, and in time, I hope we'll find that we have compatible interests. I asked you to go with me tonight because I thought it might be fun. One day I hope to see you play football even though I won't have a clue what's going on."

"You've never seen a game?" Cliff asked, sounding slightly shocked.

"I go to maybe one football game a year," Mark confessed. "I guess I prefer rugby." He threw in the remark cheekily, knowing there was some rivalry between the two teams.

Cliff caught the obvious smirk on Mark's face. He gasped dramatically and put his hand on his heart to ease the wound. "If I am ever foolish enough to introduce you to a teammate, please promise me you will never say something like that." Cliff laughed. "Why would you want to watch rugby anyway?"

Almost dismissively, Mark said, "Ah, you guys all look the same from the stands. Rugby players don't wear as much padding. They're hot." Mark smirked again for Cliff. "Next time I go to a football game, I'll pay better attention. After all, I've slept with one of the players."

"Right, I'm going to go and make *me* something to eat now." Cliff made a show of stalking off to the kitchen.

Sometimes they just felt so right together. Mark smiled at the thought. He wondered at Cliff's insecurities. *Anyone can see he's obviously intelligent.* It didn't make sense to Mark. Of course, he had to admit his own self-esteem issues were no more sensible. *What a mess. How did we ever manage to survive childhood?*

From the kitchen, Cliff shouted, "What time is this opening thing tonight?"

"It starts at seven," Mark called back.

Returning from the kitchen, a plate in each hand, Cliff said, "Maybe when your arm heals, I can teach you about football." Even after the rugby crack, he had taken pity and made a sandwich for Mark too.

Mark thought about the idea. "You mean like tossing the ball around out in a public place?"

"Yeah," Cliff replied.

"I see. That's payback for the rugby comment, isn't it?"

"No," Cliff chuckled. "I just thought it might be fun." He stood waiting, still holding the plates.

"Well, as long as you promise to be patient." Mark pictured the two of them playing around together in the sunshine. The image felt good. "I think I'd like that."

Pleased by the answer, Cliff said, "I'm looking forward to it. So, how was your day today?"

"Fine," Mark answered automatically, if a little flatly. *Oh yes, it's been a wonderfully guilt-filled day*, he thought sarcastically, *what with bumping into Dawn and then having to talk to my mother.* He sighed. Around lunchtime, Mark decided he should call his parents and let them know he wasn't going to make it down this time. His mother was disappointed yet again. "I had a little accident," he explained. "I need more time to work. No, I can't do it there." It took some convincing to quiet her fears but maintain the need to stay at school rather than go home. "I have a friend looking after me." Mark was instantly annoyed when his mom suddenly became perceptive and encouraging. The insight might be correct even if the gender was completely wrong. "Actually *he* is looking after me." Mark stressed the correction. He would need to have a talk with his parents very soon. No matter what happened between him and Cliff, his parents needed to know the real Mark.

"Oh, that bad, huh?" Cliff put a plate in front of Mark and took a seat beside him. The couch groaned a little in protest.

"Thanks." The gratitude was for the sandwich, but Mark was also thankful for the other man's concern. "No, it wasn't that bad. I guess I'm feeling a little guilty." The flicker of emotion that played over Cliff's features was almost too quick, but Mark read it easily enough. In response, he said, "I'm not feeling guilty for staying here with you. I feel guilty about hiding myself from my family."

"You know, I don't think it's fair that you can read my mind," Cliff stated semi-seriously. No one else could do that. It made him feel exposed.

"I don't think it's fair that you're at least twice as strong as I am." Mark smiled. "It puts me at the mercy of your rutting bull-moose-like self-restraint."

As if feeling the need to confirm the accuracy of Mark's assessment, Cliff put on a first-rate demonstration of both his superior strength and the suspected tenuous hold he had on his self-restraint.

Chapter 17

THE night was clear. If it hadn't been for the glow of the town, the sky would have sparkled brilliantly with stars. As it was, only the brightest stars shone through the orange haze of artificial light. Cliff had offered to drive Mark home to change. Not wanting to be late, Mark had declined.

There would've been plenty of time to stop out at Mark's place if it hadn't been for his big mouth. Not that Mark was complaining. He had been very pleased to discover that Cliff had taken the precaution of visiting the pharmacy on his way home earlier to make a few small purchases. Mark could almost still feel Cliff inside him. The sensation smoldered in his consciousness like a brand. It was a reminder that Cliff had claimed him. It gave him an odd sense of comfort. He only hoped there would be an opportunity to reciprocate later.

Mark made an effort to bring his attention back to the present. They were walking side by side in the chilly air. An easy silence fell over them on leaving the apartment. Mark felt perfectly comfortable. He remembered with amusement the pains Cliff had taken to look good for their night out. Mark, on the other hand, was wearing his same clothes from earlier. One good thing about the broken arm, he realized, was that for the convenience of dressing around it, he had gotten back into the habit of wearing button-up shirts again. Even without a change of clothes, he would be presentable for the opening tonight.

"So, Bobcat, what should I expect this evening?" Cliff asked, breaking the silence.

It surprised Mark that Cliff could appear so confident and comfortable but deep down still be insecure. It made him think about his own insecurities. "Well, Teddy Bear," Mark answered thoughtfully, "I imagine they'll serve wine in tiny plastic glasses. There will likely be trays of unidentifiable and unappetizing canapés too. People will mill about the gallery aimlessly, making intelligent-sounding conversation and not looking at the art at all. Then, later on, the artist will be introduced, who will offer some inscrutable insight into his or her work."

"And why are we doing this again?" Cliff asked with one brow raised.

Laughing, Mark tried to reassure Cliff. "Come on. It'll be interesting." Considering what he had just described, Mark wasn't surprised at Cliff's hesitation. "Openings make me a little cynical. It's too crowded to really look at the artwork. Some of the people are only there to be seen. But with luck, we'll have a chance to talk with the artist about the work. And there are some people I hope may be there." Looking at Cliff thoughtfully, Mark added, "Are you okay if I introduce you to some people?"

"Umm, sure. I guess so." Cliff reflected for a moment and then said, "Why do you ask?"

"No special reason," Mark explained. "I've got nothing up my sleeve. I was just gauging how comfortable you were with this."

"Oh." Cliff was quiet for a moment. "I guess I hadn't given it much thought." They walked on a few steps. "Well, as long as you don't introduce me as your lover, I guess that should be okay."

"Right, I'll stick with 'my friend Cliff'. But just so you know, under certain circumstances, 'friend' can be a euphemism for 'lover'." As he said this, Mark gave Cliff a look to convey his concern over the potential of accidentally outing him.

Understanding the unspoken part of the conversation, Cliff said, "Don't worry, Bobcat. I'll take my chances."

As they approached the B.A.C., it was obvious that some event was underway. Cars lined the curb and people were hurrying out of the cold to disappear through the doors in a broken but steady stream. Making their way into the building, Cliff noticed there seemed to be two distinct factions within the crowd. Oh, there were plenty of exceptions, but one part of the group was conspicuously well-dressed and distinctly older. The other part was dressed in a way that Cliff would have described as artsy. This second group seemed to be the younger attendees. Feeling distinctly out of place, he followed Mark through the crowd.

The sound of classical music filtered out from the gallery. Inside, more people were visible through the glass. Hanging their coats in a vestibule opposite the gallery, Mark asked, "Are you ready for this?" Cliff nodded in response, so Mark led the way into the fray.

Relatively speaking, the gallery was small. The size of the space wasn't the only limitation. Oversized service doors and a reception area took up one wall of the gallery. One wall was completely glass. That left two walls for hanging artwork. To get around this, moveable partitions provided extra surface area for display. The partitions also helped to create little alcoves and intimate corners out of the otherwise open space. Cliff scanned the room, but the sight was too much to take in at once. He was almost ashamed to admit he had never been in here before. Over the years, he had looked on the ever-changing displays with interest but never had the courage to enter on his own.

The room was warm with the heat of too many bodies. Mark had been right, Cliff realized. There were too many people to see the artwork properly. Cliff felt completely out of his element here. Any minute now, he was sure, someone was going to walk up and politely escort the confused and obviously lost jock politely but firmly out a side door. Unconsciously falling into step behind Mark, they crossed the room and walked directly toward a young, pretty, blonde woman standing beside the reception desk.

Mark saw Dawn immediately on entering. He approached her both relieved and apprehensive that Cliff was with him. Stopping near her, he said, "Dawn, this is my friend Cliff. Cliff, this is Dawn. Dawn is majoring in art history and works in the gallery." The two shook hands and exchanged words of greeting.

"An excellent turnout," Mark observed, wanting to make conversation.

"Yes," Dawn agreed. She politely offered the two men refreshments. Fearing that not to accept would be impolite, Cliff took one of the offered glasses. He noticed that Mark did not.

Almost immediately, someone called to Mark from the crowd. Recognizing the voice, Mark turned to Cliff and asked, "Would you like to meet my painting instructor?" Cliff only nodded. They took leave of Dawn and walked to a small group engaged in lively discussion.

Waiting only for a momentary lull in the conversation, Mark said, "Professor Robicheau, how are you this evening?"

"Ah, Mark, so good to see you." He turned politely to allow Mark to introduce his companion.

Not missing the cue, Mark said, "This is my friend, Cliff Stevens."

Cliff shook hands with the professor. He was a small man with dark, unruly hair not unlike that of a goat, but this was a person with a definite presence, Cliff assessed appreciatively.

"Nice to meet you," Professor Robicheau replied graciously. "Have you had a chance to look at the show yet?" he asked cheerfully.

Mark answered for both of them. "Not yet. We've only just arrived."

"Well, allow me to introduce the artist," the professor said with pleasure, gesturing to a woman standing within the little group. "This is Anna Patterson." The artist shook hands with the newcomers, and they exchanged pleasantries. The conversation took off again around them.

As the evening progressed, Cliff was surprised at how accepted he seemed to be here. Complete strangers engaged him in small talk. He and Mark were still moving with the same set of people clustered around the guest artist and Mark's professor. The group appeared to be the principal one in the room. People would join them while others would break away to join other, smaller clusters. They discussed an array of topics and slowly circulated through the gallery. Even the artist took time to talk with Cliff. Still, he was relieved that Mark stayed close.

After nearly an hour or so of polite conversation, Mark gently nudged Cliff toward a quiet corner containing a collection of full-height human figures made of what appeared to be rope. While outwardly examining the figures, he inquired quietly, "How are you doing?"

"Fine," Cliff replied. The novelty of the situation had kept him interested, if a bit overwhelmed.

"We can go any time," Mark assured him. "If you aren't bored yet, we could take a turn about the room and look at the artwork."

"I'd like that." Cliff was happy to stay a little longer. He was curious to get a closer look at some of the things he had glimpsed as the crowd drifted around the room. A thought occurred to him, and he asked without preamble, "Why do strangers keep walking up to me and talking to me?"

"Oh." Surprised by the question, Mark deliberated for a few seconds as he considered how best to answer. Then, speaking softly so as not to be overheard, he said, "Well, you're a striking person. It's hard to miss you. Most of the people you see here come to every single opening as well as every other snooty social event in the area. And since you've never been here before, they don't know who you are. They're curious about you." Mark hoped that made sense.

As they talked, they moved around the edge of the room and approached the piece Mark had waited to see all evening. He had purposely avoided looking for it before now because he wanted to be able to absorb the sight properly. The copper branch he had only glimpsed earlier in the day now hung from the ceiling in a glorious pool of halogen light. The spotlights changed the woven platinum leaves into iridescent fire. It was breathtaking.

While Mark admired the sight, Cliff admired the man. They were standing very close together. Mark was so handsome in his eyes. Cliff reluctantly spared some of his attention to examine the metal sculpture.

It was beautiful. "It's hard to believe this is metal. It doesn't seem solid at all. I almost want to touch it."

"Exactly what I had hoped to achieve," said a voice behind them. The artist had joined them silently with Dawn at her side.

"I knew this was the one that would get all your attention." The comment Dawn directed toward Mark carried a measure of bitterness. She was glancing at Cliff as she said it. "Please excuse me," she said to Anna, and left them without another word.

The chill lasted a few seconds until Mark shook it off by asking Anna a question about her artwork. They walked and chatted with the artist for a few minutes until she was compelled to join another group.

"Bobcat, what was that about?" Cliff asked.

For a fleeting moment, Mark considered being evasive, but he knew what Cliff was asking. He answered very quietly. "Dawn had a crush on me. I didn't know. After I figured it out, I told her I was gay." *What more was there to say? Oh, yes.* "She's jealous of you."

Time appeared to stand still. It was as if the outside world was perversely determined to intrude on Cliff's little fantasy. For one week, he thought he could have Mark and yet keep up the illusion of the straight athlete. *No! I don't care.* He didn't care what anyone thought. He was not giving up Mark.

"Should we go?" Mark asked gently.

"No," Cliff answered resolutely. "I want you to show me the other pieces."

Mark led the way. He glanced around the room but didn't see Dawn in the crowd. Mark wished he could talk to her. *It won't do any good.* Dawn would have to realize that this was who he was, and he couldn't change.

By the time they reached the hemp figures again, the artist rejoined them. Anna gave the impression of being relieved. "Openings are always like this," she sighed. She practically hid behind Cliff, using his bulk to block her from the view of the other guests. "I can only

THE LAST SNOW OF WINTER

handle so much." She looked to Cliff and asked, "How are you enjoying it all?"

"Your work is amazing," Cliff replied, feeling a little on the spot.

"No, I meant the show," Anna whispered conspiratorially, and made a hand motion to indicate the people around them.

"Oh, well, this is all new to me," Cliff said after he realized what she was asking. "Mark is introducing me to the art world."

Anna smiled at that. Looking to Mark, she said, "Wayne tells me your work is quite promising."

"He's being generous." Turning to Cliff, Mark explained, "Wayne is Professor Robicheau."

"I doubt that," Anna replied in response to Mark's dismissal of the praise. After a glance across the room, she added, "I'm sorry to run, but I need to make a quick getaway. It was nice to meet you both." She shook their hands and fled.

"Is it always like this?" Cliff asked.

"Yeah." Mark made the observation with a tone of comfortable resignation. "You should have been here a few months ago. The woman in the red dress, you see, there." He pointed her out. "I don't know her name. She was all over me." He added ruefully, "I only seem to attract women." Mark felt a sudden pang of guilt on remembering Dawn.

"You attracted me," Cliff reminded him. The sound of his voice was deep and sexy.

"Easy, big guy," Mark cautioned. "We're in a very public place."

"Maybe we should fix that," Cliff rumbled suggestively.

Outside again, the night looked the same. Only the temperature had changed. The freezing air exaggerated the echo of their footsteps.

"Thanks for taking me," Cliff said after they had walked a few minutes in silence.

"Thanks for agreeing to come," Mark replied. "I told you it would be interesting."

"That it was, Bobcat. Now let's go home." It had been an educational evening. Cliff was glad to have experienced it, but he was ready to be home where they could relax in private. Encouraged by the weather, they walked quickly. It was a relief when they finally arrived at the apartment and were able to get out of the cold and shed their winter clothes.

"I'm going to change," Cliff said as he moved toward the bedroom. Within minutes, he returned wearing shorts and another well-worn T-shirt. He held up a little bundle of clothes and inquired invitingly, "Care to join me?"

Curious, Mark agreed and accepted the offered clothing. Cliff helped him remove his own things. The items selected for him were the same shorts from before and a football jersey that was too large. It fit very loosely. Mark felt a little ridiculous in it. He faced Cliff and said, "I feel like a six-year-old wearing his father's shirt."

"Well, I figured you would be more comfortable, and it would be easy to get on and off." Cliff looked Mark up and down appraisingly, taking in the overall effect. "I have to admit, it's a bit of a turn-on to see you in my clothes."

That was a surprise. "Would you rather that I was into sports?" Mark asked, somewhat uneasy.

"No. That wasn't what I was getting at," Cliff replied. "I guess I like the idea of you being mine." He opened his arms, indicating that Mark should cuddle up next to him.

Mark did so but didn't say anything.

It was impossible for Cliff to miss the effect his remark had had. Mark was obviously lost in his own thoughts. "I've offended you." It was a statement rather than a question. The words brought Mark back to the room.

"No, I was just considering what you said about belonging to you," he said. "The idea doesn't feel like... submission. It's a surprise to discover that I could be yours easily."

It was Cliff's turn to be silent. His proposition that they give over a single week to this fantasy was beginning to feel like a huge mistake. How was he ever going to let go at the end of it?

They could have talked about the evening. They could have talked about anything, but they were both lost in their own separate worlds.

Chapter 18

THE dim light creeping in past the gaps in the blind hinted at the dull and gloomy sky outside. Cliff had been awake several minutes but didn't make a move to get up. Mark was nestled close, and Cliff watched him sleep. Eventually they had talked on the couch. Each of them had made an effort to cast off their respective reveries. The conversation moved to the bedroom, where they eventually fell asleep. Their talk had been safe, a retreat position. They each saw the flaw in the bargain they had made, but for the sake of the other, neither was ready to face it. Cliff knew it was already too late for him. His bobcat may or may not be truly his, but there was no question that he loved Mark.

A change in the pattern of Mark's breathing alerted Cliff that he was waking. His lover shifted beside him. With no easy solution at hand, Cliff fell back to the axiom that served him well. *There's nothing for it.* "Morning, Bobcat," he said when Mark tentatively opened an eyelid.

Still sleepy, Mark answered by saying, "Good morning, my big teddy bear." This was what he wanted, to wake up in the morning next to his teddy bear.

"I'm going to the gym this morning," Cliff informed. "And we have plans this evening. What do you have on the agenda for today?"

"Back to the library for me," Mark sighed in reply. "I'm working on a paper for Taxonomy. Some of the books I've been digging out of the library haven't been checked out since the forties."

"Sounds cutting edge," Cliff commented.

Playing along, Mark said, "I'm mapping out changes in taxonomic nomenclature over time as discoveries were made about the organisms in question." Mark let his voice drone as he spieled it out.

Cliff laughed. "Do let me read that some time."

"Yeah, like psychology is so much better." Mark made an effort to tickle the bigger man. Cliff made short work of pinning him down. "Not fair!" he complained.

Rolling to place himself completely on top of Mark, Cliff began kissing the smaller man's neck hungrily. He pulled back to see Mark's face. "You were saying."

"You big moose," Mark teased.

"My little bobcat," Cliff replied sweetly.

If waking up next to someone you loved was what Mark had always wanted, this must be the gravy. His big bear of a lover was playful and delightfully randy. Mark pushed his erection suggestively against the man holding him down. Cliff responded with a lust-filled growl. Mornings were good.

ALONE in the gym, Cliff pushed himself through repetitions almost in a trance. The activities of the morning replayed in his head. Had someone been there to point it out to him, Cliff wouldn't have been that surprised to discover he was grinning goofily.

It was early afternoon when Cliff found himself walking past the imposing columned facade of U Hall. Mark was probably still in the computer lab, he realized. He knew he should let the man work undisturbed but couldn't resist seeing him. Telling himself he would just check in on Mark, Cliff made for the upper entrance of the B.A.C.

The campus was relatively deserted, not empty but still quiet. The people he passed were unfamiliar to him. Impatient to see Mark again, Cliff took the stairs to the lower level quickly, two at a time. The glassed-in computer lab was just ahead. Ah, there was his bobcat, but not alone. A sudden surge of jealousy threatened to engulf Cliff.

Through the windows, Cliff could see Mark leaning back in his chair, apparently in comfortable conversation with a tall man opposite. The tall man was half-sitting against the edge of the computer desk. Both men were smiling and laughing. With a considerable effort, Cliff calmed himself and pushed the door to the lab open.

Noticing Cliff enter, Mark's face became even brighter. Cliff didn't return the smile. He had unconsciously retreated into his defensive mask. The unknown man took leave of Mark and made a friendly nod to Cliff as he passed him, heading for the exit.

Waiting only for the door to close, Mark said quietly, "Hey, Teddy Bear."

"Hey." Cliff felt the need to say more. "Did you eat?"

"My usual," Mark replied easily. "I picked up an apple and some almonds at Wade's."

"Was that Wade?" The question came out in a conspicuously cool tone.

"What?" Mark paused to consider Cliff's odd behavior. "Wade's, you know, the grocery store downtown." All of a sudden, the pieces neatly fell into place. Mark explained in a carefully even tone, "That was Jonathan. We're classmates. And he's straight." Letting the information sink in for a few seconds, Mark then asked, "Is that why you steamed in here in full tough-guy mode?"

Feeling foolish, Cliff only made an inarticulate noise in reply.

Mark mulled over the situation. "I suppose I should feel flattered. Except that it suggests you don't trust me. Or you feel I can't take care of myself."

"It was stupid. I'm sorry." The shame he felt at overreacting was making it difficult for Cliff to drop his defenses.

Mark seemed to understand and thoughtfully changed the subject. "How was your workout?" he asked as a way of easing the tension.

"I kept thinking about you," Cliff admitted.

"What am I going to do with you, you big moose?" Mark asked, half-serious.

"You could spank me," Cliff spat out and then instantly regretted the joke.

"I just might." Mark shook his head and then asked, "You heading home?"

"Yeah, I wanted to check on you. You know, before I made a fool of myself." Cliff was starting to relax. It had been a stupid reaction, but they would get past it.

"I'll need to go to my place and change before we head off to your professor's." Mark was happy to see the real Cliff, his Cliff, reappearing from behind the mask. "Will you be able to give me a hand?"

Plans made for later, Cliff anxiously scanned the corridor outside the lab before bending to give Mark a kiss goodbye. It was risky, but he felt the need to have some physical connection after his regrettable behavior. With almost no outward sign of surprise, Mark gratefully accepted the kiss.

Alone at home, Cliff plodded through page after page of dry text. He was about to give up when he heard the sound of someone thumping up the stairs outside. It was his turn to brighten when he saw it was Mark.

Mark let himself in. Seeing Cliff's face, he returned the other man's smile easily. It was amazing how much joy he felt in seeing his big teddy bear. After all, it had only been a few hours since the kiss in the lab. The hug Cliff gave him was a little too forceful, but Mark didn't mind. He liked the way his big bear got carried away. "You miss me?"

"Not really," Cliff lied.

"We should get going," Mark said. Right then, he would have been happy to forget all about their plans for dinner.

Cliff groaned but obediently collected his boots and pulled them on. "You know, we wouldn't have to leave so soon if we took my car." They had already discussed this, but Mark insisted on walking. Cliff didn't really mind, but he enjoyed giving his lover a hard time.

There was no need to rush on their way out to Mark's cottage. They had plenty of time. As they walked, they exchanged occasional observations about things they saw and talked pleasantly about nothing in particular. Cliff had never been big on walking as a pastime, but he enjoyed the private time spent with Mark.

Before Cliff would have believed it possible, they arrived at the cottage. It seemed like they had just stepped out the door, yet here they were. Cliff noticed a note taped to the glass of Mark's front door. He plucked the note off and held it for Mark, who was again struggling to get his keys. "Why don't you keep them in your left pocket?" he asked, exasperated and amused at the same time.

"I forgot," Mark replied. "What's the note say?"

Not expecting it to be anything important, Cliff unfolded the paper and read it aloud. "Mark, I made plans with your mom to surprise you by picking you up at the train station yesterday. How dare you not show? Call me. Talk to you soon, David. PS. Get a damn phone, you loser. D."

Mark laughed at the postscript. That was David. *How did he get that note here?*

"Who is this?" Cliff asked. Once they were inside, he handed the message over.

"That's my friend David," Mark explained. "He's the one who's afraid some big bad football player is going to leave me in a ditch one day. Wait 'til he sees you."

Cliff made a noncommittal sound. "Maybe you should call him now. We might be late."

"No good. Dave won't even be home before midnight." Mark took off his jacket. "He's a bit of a night owl. Are we staying at your place tonight?"

"It's closer," Cliff reasoned. "Besides, I hate your shower. And your bed is too small."

"Well, in that case, I need to take a change of clothes with me," Mark decided.

"I like it when you wear my clothes." The tone of Cliff's voice was very thoughtful. He continued by saying, "I wish we could just lock the door and curl up in bed together."

Mark had been about to explain that he couldn't very well wear Cliff's clothes out in public but said instead, "We can do that sometime." He found Cliff's sentiment touching.

"You know what I mean, Bobcat."

It did seem like the outside world was intent on breaking up their little party. They just needed to find a way to bring the two sides together. *If only it were that easy,* Mark thought. He stepped into the bedroom with Cliff in tow.

Changed and carrying clean socks and underwear in a pocket of his book bag, Mark locked the door and turned to Cliff. "Nervous?"

"Yup," Cliff replied immediately. "You?"

"Oh yeah."

"Great!" Cliff said. "Let's go."

Chapter 19

Dr. Hansen lived in a low, relatively modern, ranch-style house. From the architectural details of the exterior, Mark estimated it dated back to the sixties. He was curious how it had come to be here on this street, nestled in amongst century-old Victorian houses. He and Cliff stood in the muted glow cast by the glass block sidelights that framed the entrance. From the other side of the attractively grained and substantial-looking wooden door, they could hear the sound of a dog barking. By the timbre and the relatively slow repetition of the barks, Mark guessed it was a mid- to large-size dog. There was no message of danger in the barking. Mark was at ease about that. The dog was only alerting his pack to the presence of strangers. The barking had started as soon as Cliff had touched the doorbell. It was an effective arrangement, Mark mused happily. The humor helped distract him from the nervousness he was feeling.

When the door opened, warm light from the bright foyer washed over them. An athletic-looking woman stood there in the glare, awkwardly restraining a gleaming brown lab with one hand. "Cliff," she said warmly, greeting him with an open smile. Her voice barely carried over the commotion of the dog. "Mini, enough," she pleaded with the dog.

Now able to examine the intruders, Mini became much more pliable. The task of protecting her pack complete, she sat expectantly by her master, watching the visitors to see what would happen next.

"Hi, Carla," Cliff said as he was welcomed with a hug. He took a step back and turned to Mark, "Bobcat, this is Carla Hansen." The accidental use of the pet name caused Cliff to redden visibly.

Mark took the offered hand in his left and explained pleasantly, "Cliff calls me Bobcat. My name is Mark Poole. Either is fine."

"I think I will call you Mark for now," the woman said with a small smile. "Call me Carla. And this young lady," Carla indicated the glossy brown form now sitting meekly by the door, "is Minerva. We call her Mini, for short." As if given leave, Mini approached Mark. He greeted her by stroking her elegant head. "Let me take your coats," Carla offered graciously.

Having shed their winter clothes, they followed Carla into a comfortable living room. "Can I get you something to drink?" Both men politely declined the offer. "Theo should just be a few minutes. Please sit while I check on dinner." Mini had followed the group into the room and strategically positioned herself next to Mark.

Within minutes of sitting down, a man joined them from the hallway. Cliff stood automatically to make the introductions. Mark politely rose also. "Mark, this is Dr. Hansen, my mentor. Dr. Hansen, this is my friend Mark."

"It is a pleasure to meet you," Dr. Hansen said as he shook Mark's left hand. "Call me Ted. Cliff told me about your arm. How is it now?"

"It's much better," Mark replied. "I'm looking forward to getting rid of the sling."

They each took a seat. "You may not know this, but Carla is a nutritionist," Ted said to Mark conversationally. "I hope you like tofu and lentils."

"I heard that," Carla shouted from the kitchen. She immediately joined them in the living room and balanced on the arm of the chair where her husband was sitting. "Dinner is almost ready," she announced. Then addressing Mark, she said, "I understand you're not a psychology student."

"No, I'm working on a Bachelor of Science in biology," Mark answered.

"Excellent." Carla seemed remarkably satisfied with the information. She turned to her husband beside her but said for Mark's benefit, "Dinner conversation in this house is often dominated by a single subject... or person." She kissed her husband lightly on the forehead to soften the rebuke. He accepted the gentle warning and kiss good-naturedly.

They seemed like such a loving couple. Mark felt quite at home with them.

The sound of a single chime pierced the air. Carla rose and returned to the kitchen. Ted followed to help her with the final preparations for dinner. Minutes later, they invited their guests to take seats in the adjoining dining room. Over a first course of squash and curry soup, the two couples got to know each other better. To Mark, the entire situation felt like being invited to sit at the grownups' table for the first time. He secretly hoped he was up to the demands.

Dinner was delightful. The food was tasty. There was indeed a course of lentils and tofu. The conversation was sparkling and varied. It was obvious that the Hansens were well-read and held a variety of interests. Despite Carla's prediction, psychology didn't dominate the table. Mark hadn't known what to expect but was pleased to find he was having a wonderful time.

After a dessert of fresh fruit, they returned to the living room. Carla stepped into the kitchen to prepare the tea, and Cliff excused himself to visit the washroom. While Cliff had known and been friends with his mentor for some time, he had never dined with Ted and Carla before. He hadn't been prepared for such a thoroughly enjoyable evening. That they appeared to approve of Mark was a relief. Why he felt relieved, though, Cliff wasn't certain.

Now alone in the living room with Mark, Dr. Hansen took the opportunity to say a few words in confidence. "I would like to say that I am extremely pleased that Cliff has found someone like you."

Feeling slightly self-conscious and uncertain how to respond, Mark simply nodded.

"He seems so different tonight. It's good to see him so happy." Ted considered the change in his student and friend. "It's obvious that he cares for you profoundly."

"He was rather talking me up earlier," Mark admitted shyly. During dinner, Mark had blushed more than once at Cliff's overheated praise for his artwork.

Ted nodded and said, "He's a good man." At the sound of a door opening in the hallway, Ted respectfully dropped the subject. While Cliff was seating himself, Ted said to Mark, "I understand you intend to become a veterinarian."

"Yes," Mark replied.

"To please your parents," Ted said.

Mark shot a glance toward Cliff.

Tea tray in hand, Carla joined them from the kitchen. "Theo." The tone of her voice carried a subtle note of warning.

Clearing his throat quietly, Mark acknowledged the truth in the observation. "Yes, I have to admit that deep down I'm motivated by a desire to make them proud of me." He had spoken the words formally.

"Yet you can see the danger there." Dr. Hansen noted. "You don't think they would be proud of you as an artist?"

Cliff shifted uncomfortably in his seat. These were his very own opinions that he had shared with Ted yesterday, but he could see that the discussion was making Mark uneasy.

"I think...." Mark paused and considered the relationship he had with his parents. Objectively he could believe they would understand. "I hope they would be proud of me no matter what. I'm just not so sure I'm good enough to make it as an artist. Maybe I'm not talented enough." Mark felt Cliff's hand press against his own. The contact was a comfort.

Dr. Hansen reflected thoughtfully on Mark's words for a few seconds. "Fear can make us do or not do many things. There are times when we should take chances and pursue our dreams." He turned to face Cliff. "And there are times when we have to be realistic and face facts. Sometimes we just need a friend to give us a little push in the right direction." After a brief pause, he turned back to Mark and asked, "Has Cliff told you anything about his football injuries?"

The abrupt change in direction threw Mark. He had been feeling persecuted but now wasn't so sure. Confusion prevented him from forming an answer.

"Theo," Carla said. The tone was different this time and conveyed a message that Mark didn't pick up on. She rose and made a show of serving the tea, sparing a recriminating glance for her husband that Mark did catch. Ted only shrugged slightly and accepted a cup. Conversation resumed but didn't sparkle as it had earlier.

The evening wound down. The four of them plus Mini crowded the foyer as Mark and Cliff put on their winter clothes. Pleasantries exchanged, thanks given, and a genuine desire for a repeat of the evening expressed on all sides, they parted.

Outside, alone, the two men walked silently. Cliff wondered what Mark might be thinking. He had been quiet for the latter part of the evening. In the silence, Cliff became more and more withdrawn himself. Not a word passed between them until they reached the corner of Cliff's street. Cliff noticed hesitation in the man beside him and thought he saw a fleeting glance up the street in the direction they had been walking. "Would you rather go home?" he asked.

It took a moment for Mark to understand what he had heard. He was so lost in his own woolgathering he barely remembered anything that had passed since they had stepped out into the cold. Blinking and looking into the eyes of his companion, Mark could see Cliff was wearing his game face again. "I'd rather stay with you," he answered honestly. "I'm sorry, I wasn't very good company for the walk."

"Where were you?" Cliff asked, unconsciously relaxing his defenses. They turned and continued up the side street together.

"I was thinking about what Dr. Hansen said about pleasing my parents." It was true. Mark wanted his parents to be proud of him. "The irony is that I've been so afraid they would discover my secret and

THE LAST SNOW OF WINTER

disown me that I've preemptively distanced myself from them. We barely have a relationship." He shook his head without being aware of it.

"Do you want to talk about it?" Cliff asked.

As they climbed the stairs, Mark said," Do you really think I should become an artist rather than a vet?" Not waiting for an answer, he also asked, "Why didn't you say anything to me?"

That was fair. Yeah, he should've said something to Mark. "Let's get comfortable first," Cliff said as he unlocked the door.

Wearing the borrowed jersey again, Mark thoughtfully stroked the satiny fabric. He was grateful to have convinced Cliff that he could do without the sling for a few hours. Curled up at one end of the couch, Mark waited for Cliff. The bigger man apparently needed a snack after a vegetarian dinner. The fact amused Mark.

Cliff returned from the kitchen carrying a sandwich. He was wearing a T-shirt and shorts. Holding up the sandwich, he said, "Promise not to tell Carla."

Chuckling, Mark replied, "You know when you flash those beautiful blue eyes at me, I would agree to anything."

Sitting down, Cliff cocked his head to the side and studied Mark thoughtfully. "I wore that when I played in high school," he said, indicating the jersey. "It's too small for me now, but I keep it because it means a lot to me." He considered why he liked seeing Mark in it. Maybe it was a sign of possession. Maybe he wanted to tie together the things that were important to him.

It would be very easy to get comfortable and forget all about the world around them. Some part of Mark wanted to do just that. *Who cares about parents and mentors?* They only had a few days to play at this, and then who knew what would happen? Mark shivered. *How will I ever go back to my old life?*

Cliff had been eating quietly, glancing occasionally at his companion. Mark was becoming quiet again, obviously falling deeper into thought. Wanting to head it off, he said, "It didn't seem like something I could say to you. We had just met, and I didn't want to sound like I was telling you what to do."

The abrupt change in topic caused Mark some confusion until he recalled the conversation from the street. "But you talked with Dr. Hansen about it."

"Ted is probably my closest friend right now," Cliff explained. "He has been a mentor to me in every way. When I told him about us, it just came out."

"I understand. I guess I was a little taken aback by the questioning." Recalling the exchange, Mark asked, "What did he mean about your football injuries?"

Cliff was sure he knew precisely what his mentor had intended. "I don't think Ted was targeting you with his interrogation." Mark gave him a questioning look, so Cliff continued by saying, "We have a slight disagreement about my career. I think he was using the subject to remind me of that. And maybe sabotage me."

"Sabotage you?" Mark asked. "How so?"

"By bringing you alongside," Cliff replied.

"I don't understand."

"I've had a number of injuries on the field." There were almost too many for Cliff to recall, at least the minor ones. However, there were a few significant ones. "I've had sprains, torn ligaments, broken bones. It can be a rough game, and I've played it hard."

Mark listened in a thoughtful silence. It was easy enough to believe that football could be a brutal sport. He didn't like the idea of Cliff getting hurt, but he was doing something he enjoyed.

"I've had a few concussions." Cliff watched Mark for his reaction. His lover absorbed the information and waited. Cliff knew this was what Ted had had in mind when he'd introduced the subject. Ted wanted Cliff to spell out the significance of his injuries to Mark. In doing so, Cliff would have to reflect on their significance too. Not to mention look his lover in the eye while doing it. His voice became clinical as he said, "The effects of a concussion on the brain are suspected to be cumulative. Subsequent concussions may lead to an elevated risk of brain impairment. There's also a possibility that, having experienced a concussion, a person becomes more susceptible to them in the future. And it seems I'm naturally sensitive." Cliff didn't mention the scare he'd had last fall. The temporary memory loss that lingered for days had prompted the team doctor to send him to a neurologist in Halifax.

There was a space of time where nothing seemed to happen. Mark looked away from Cliff. His eyes became unfocused as he reflected on what he was hearing. Eventually Mark asked, "So, there's a chance you may suffer a permanent brain injury?"

"Yeah, that is possible," Cliff admitted reluctantly.

Mark was having trouble relating. *There are risks in every profession*, he reminded himself. Yes, that was true. Police officers, firefighters, practically every job had inherent risks. Mark had once been pinned to a wall by a thousand plus pounds of solid horse while assisting the vet on a routine call. The incident had only left him with bruised ribs and a sore back but could have been more serious. It was the same, except that football was just a game. He asked aloud, "Playing a game?"

Feeling defensive, Cliff stated, "It's a game I love. It's what I do." Surely, Mark could understand how important this was to him.

The defensive air was easy for Mark to detect. He didn't want Cliff to feel he was being attacked. "Dr. Hansen wants you to give up football, then?"

"That's not precisely true," Cliff replied slowly. "Ted wants me to reexamine my career options." Mark didn't prod, but Cliff could see he was waiting for clarification. "The chances of anyone getting to play pro are pretty slim. I'm the first to admit I'm not a star player. I'm good but not exceptional. I've also taken a few too many injuries and been put out of too many games because of them. I'm not a good prospect."

Mark massaged his forehead with his fingertips. "I'm confused. It sounds like you're saying you don't think you'll ever play professionally, but you still try?"

Cliff let out a rush of air that ended almost with a sigh. "I'm never going to play pro. I know that. I just don't know how to give up. It's what I've worked for since...." He fell silent.

Reaching out, Mark took Cliff's hand. Compared to his own, Cliff's hand looked massive. It was such a strong hand. How could he hope to help this big man? "I don't have any answers. I can't tell you what to do. But I'll love you no matter what."

Drawing in a shattered breath, Cliff could feel the power in what Mark was offering. He couldn't speak past the lump in his throat, not yet. His eyes dropped to the hand holding his. Mark's fingers were long and tapered. The hand was graceful, sensitive, an artist's hand. The artist was doing what his family expected just to please them. *And what am I doing? I'm blindly following a path to a dead end. Are we both fools?*

They didn't say anything for a few minutes. Having restored some sense of calm, Cliff asked, "Have you ever considered becoming a professional artist?"

"Yes," Mark admitted, "I've considered it."

"What stopped you?"

"Fear," Mark answered without having to think about it. "My father, my grandfather, my uncles and cousins, they're all fishermen. They're solid, simple, hardworking people. I like them, but I've never fit in with them. Finding out I'm gay will be hard enough for my family, but I know I can't change that. Not following in my father's footsteps, well, that's an insult. I want him to be proud. I know I can be a good vet. What if I'm not good enough to be a successful artist?"

"You're confusing what you are with what you do." As he said the words, Cliff realized they hit a little close to home. Cliff squeezed Mark's hand kindly. "I don't have any answers either, Bobcat. But I'll love you no matter what."

THE LAST SNOW OF WINTER

With no energy to say more, they sat quietly for a while. Eventually they prepared for bed. Mark lay on his left side so he could see Cliff. Cliff lay facing Mark, running his hand gently down Mark's injured arm over and over. In time, they fell asleep.

Chapter 20

Waking first, Cliff slipped out of bed to make a visit to the bathroom. By the light coming in past the gaps in the blind, it looked like it would be a nice day. He returned to the bed as quietly as he could, but Mark woke as he tried to climb in next to him.

Mark yawned and blinked his eyes a few times to clear his vision. He then focused on Cliff's face and smiled.

The look Mark gave him warmed Cliff's heart to almost burning. So gentle and so beautiful was his lover. *And he loves you*, Cliff reminded himself. "Do you want to know why I call you Bobcat?"

"Tell me." Mark was very curious.

"I was born and grew up in Mississauga," Cliff explained, getting comfortable next to his lover. "Every summer I was shipped off to my grandparents' place for a few weeks." Cliff had resented the separation from his friends at the time but now remembered the visits fondly. "There's a wildlife park not far from where they lived. When I was younger, I pestered my grandparents to take me. Then one summer when I was a little older, I don't remember what started it, but I was determined to see every single animal in the park.

"See, no matter how many times I went, there were always enclosures that seemed to be empty. I became suspicious that they really were empty." Cliff remembered feeling cheated. He even accused one of the keepers of the deception. "I was old enough to go on my own then. I went every day I could and stayed as long as possible. I made a list and checked each animal off as I saw it." Mark pictured a young Cliff doggedly on task, an early version of his stern bearing on a young boy's face. The mental image made him smile.

"After a few days, some of the staff took pity on me and let me sneak in without paying." That was a blessing. He had nearly used all his allowance paying the admittance fee. "It wasn't long before the entire staff knew my goal. A worker found me one day standing in front of one of the enclosures. He asked what I was looking for. I explained, and he laughed. He crouched beside me and pointed to a dark shape on a branch. There it was. I had missed it all this time. A bobcat was there, silently watching me.

"Joe, the zookeeper who showed me the bobcat, took me under his wing. I became his helper, and in exchange, he taught me about the animals. He even let me come in after hours so I could help with feeding. I saw every animal that summer, but my favorite was the bobcat. She seemed so small and beautiful. At night, I sometimes fell asleep dreaming about taking her home. She could live with me away from the cage and be free." Cliff shook his head at his young self's innocence.

"I got to see her up close one day. She was waiting for her meal by the food lock. She was still beautiful but not as small as I thought. From a distance, she seemed so quiet and tame, always inconspicuous, quietly observing everything. From close-up, I finally realized she wasn't a pet. Separated by thin metal bars, I could sense she was powerful and dangerous. I could respect her but not possess her." Cliff hoped Mark would understand. He stroked the fine hairs that circled the other man's belly button but didn't meet his eyes.

Mark reflected on what Cliff had said. "Thank you."

"I didn't notice you at first," Cliff confessed. "We had been in the same classes for months before I caught you watching me. The feeling it gave me reminded me of that first encounter with the bobcat. I studied you after that. You observe everything, everyone, unobtrusively." There was a depth and stillness about Mark that Cliff found soothing. There was also a strength and self-sufficiency about the man. He respected that. "You already know what happened next."

"You imagined taking me home?" The tease was a gentle counter to the serious mood of the admission.

"Something like that," Cliff replied, appreciating the effort. "Then I got to know you. You appear so quiet and pliable, but underneath there's a will of steel. My bobcat."

The nickname had felt strange at first. With repetition and now appreciating the sentiment, Mark could accept it. "Thank you for telling me."

They stayed together under the covers for a while. Not wanting to break the spell, Mark resisted the persistent urgings of his bladder as long as he could. Eventually he had to give in. He was surprised when Cliff wordlessly followed him to the bathroom. Mark tried desperately to relax and relieve himself as Cliff prepared the shower. Realizing his presence was giving Mark a shy bladder, Cliff clicked his tongue and stepped out of the room. Bladder finally empty, Mark called Cliff back in so they could shower together.

The hot water felt good as they explored each other's bodies under its flow. They took their time, not rushing the experience like before. Eventually touching and exploring escalated to heated breathing and hands roaming over and roughly groping each other. Cliff took the lead, kneeling down and taking Mark's swollen cock in his mouth. Wanting to let Mark know that he considered turnabout fair play, he took Mark's load deep in his throat, splashing his own cum over his lover's feet.

Just the memory of the sight of his muscled bear of a lover eagerly accepting his cock would be enough for Mark to get off in the future. Though he hoped there would be more scenes like that one. Sex in the shower left Mark feeling spent and a little overheated. Once dried, he passively followed Cliff to the bedroom and sat on the edge of the bed. Feeling utterly relaxed, he was tempted to curl up and fall back to sleep.

"Come on, my lazy little bobcat. You can't sleep all day." Cliff tossed Mark's clothes onto his lap. "What are your plans for today?"

"Back to the computer lab for a while," Mark sighed. "I'm almost finished with my taxonomy paper. After that, I'm going to the studio to paint." Despite his arm, he was looking forward to making an attempt at painting. It had been days since he'd been in the studio. *Too long.*

Curious to see more of Mark's artwork, Cliff immediately asked, "Can I stop by? You promised to show me your work."

"Sure," Mark agreed easily. "I'd like that. And what are your plans for today?"

"I've got to pick up some papers at U Hall. Then reading, reading, and more reading," Cliff groaned. "I'm a little behind."

"I like your behind."

Cliff laughed. "If you're good, I may let you play with it later. Now let's get some breakfast. I'm starving."

It was indeed a sunny day. Just nice enough to believe that spring was almost here. Chances were that there would be at least one more snowstorm this season, but that was no reason not to enjoy the fine weather. The two men walked side by side in the sunshine.

On the way to campus, Mark stopped at the grocery store to pick up his usual lunch of a Granny Smith apple and a little bag of roasted almonds from the bulk section. Cliff rolled his eyes on seeing the meager meal. Noticing the look, Mark laughed and informed him, "I eat a good breakfast and a good supper. I don't need that much at lunch. Besides, when I get painting, I often forget to eat anyway. Not to mention everything else."

"I'll remember that," said Cliff.

On entering the B.A.C., Mark pointed out a pair of unmarked and unremarkable doors in an alcove just past the gallery. "Through there," he indicated to Cliff. "Take a right and then a left. The studios are on the right side of the corridor. I'll be in the first one, probably sometime after lunch."

Cliff had never noticed the doors before even though he had a class just across the way. "Okay, I'll see you later." The urge to give

Mark a goodbye kiss struck him. The presence of people nearby prohibited the action. He hated this.

Mark seemed to understand. "It's okay. I'll see you later." He walked away casually, seemingly unaffected.

Frozen to the spot and watching Mark leave, Cliff felt torn. He shook off the feeling of conflict and started out on his errands.

Chapter 21

AS THE day passed, a skewed rectangle of sunlight slowly crawled from one side of the living room to the other. Cliff hardly noticed. He had been reading for hours, making notes and occasionally changing his position on the couch. His body felt stiff from the long period of physical inactivity. He stretched and yawned. Setting his book aside, he decided it was time for a break. The glass of tulips on the coffee table caught his eye. The petals were fully open now. The stems arched gracefully as the flowers followed the sunlight across the room. Checking his watch, Cliff decided it was a good time to visit Mark.

The walk to campus was uneventful. With most of the students away, the town had a distinctly sleepy feel. Cliff reached the B.A.C. without passing a single person he knew. On entering the building, he crossed purposely to the doors that led to the studios and pushed past them. Beyond the doors, the architecture changed noticeably. This area was much less finished than the more public spaces of the building, or at least much less refined. The walls were raw, unpainted cinderblock. The ceiling height soared into the exposed steel structure that supported the floor above. The doors lining the corridor were double height. The combination of the oversized doors and the high ceiling made the relatively narrow corridor feel even taller. The overall effect was a little oppressive.

Cliff felt out of place in the unfamiliar surroundings but moved on resolutely. He could hear music coming from somewhere ahead. An open door further along the corridor appeared to be the source of the sound. *That must be the studio*, he reasoned. Sure enough, it was. He stepped through the tall opening into a bright, sunlit room. The music was louder here, something classical Cliff didn't recognize. It was moody, deep, and slow, like the movement of the tide.

The studio was a large, open space, lit by skylights. It smelled of oil paint and contained an abundance of things arranged with no rhyme or reason that Cliff could fathom. The room so overwhelmed his senses that it took a few minutes for him to notice Mark.

Mark gave no sign that he had heard someone come in. He was standing, his back to Cliff, in front of a large canvas. Curious, Cliff watched him silently. Mark appeared to be in a sort of trance. He moved slowly, deliberately, considering and examining the canvas with obvious intensity, now touching the brush he held in his left hand to a palette placed on a stool beside him and then lifting the brush to the canvas. The brush deposited its pigments, making subtle changes to the image. The process was almost hypnotic.

Not wanting to startle the man, Cliff waited until Mark stepped back from the canvas again. When he did, Cliff called softly, "Bobcat?" Mark didn't start on hearing the sound. He only turned slowly to face Cliff. The look in his eyes was at first remote but warmed quickly with recognition.

Coming out of the trance, Mark said with a smile, "Hey, Teddy Bear." His voice came out gravelly, as if it hadn't been used in a while. "What time is it?"

"It's a quarter to five," Cliff said, looking to his watch. Wanting to examine the painting his lover had been so intent on, he stepped forward to stand behind Mark. Cliff placed his hands on either side of Mark's waist and held him close to look over his shoulder at the image on the canvas. Warmth radiated from Mark's body.

The subject of the painting was a fox. It moved through tall, windswept grass on a hillside. An ocean vista was visible on the horizon behind the fox. The greens were lush and sunny, but the ocean felt moody like the music.

Letting Cliff have time to take it in, Mark waited and then said, "This is a final project for the course. The professor wanted to encourage us to work big. I have a tendency to work small and focus on detail. One good thing about not having the use of my right arm: I have to paint loosely and not get hung up on the details."

Cliff could see what he was saying. The brush strokes were clearly visible. It didn't look as refined as the two paintings Cliff had seen at Mark's cottage, but it had more energy. A sound from the direction of the door broke the spell. Cliff looked up to see someone standing there. He automatically let go of Mark and took a step back.

"Sorry to intrude," Professor Robicheau said in apology. "I just wanted to see how you were fairing, Mark. But I'll leave you to it." The professor turned the way he'd come. "Don't forget to lock up," he reminded over his shoulder, casually waving as he stepped into the hall.

Mark faced Cliff. The big man wore a look of guilt "Are you okay? Professor Robicheau doesn't care."

"I know," Cliff replied. "It just feels like things are unraveling too fast."

"I'm sorry."

"It's not your fault. I'm the one who keeps forgetting to be careful." Cliff was beginning to wonder if some part of him wanted to get caught. Putting that aside, he asked, "Tell me about this painting?"

Choosing to let the incident go, Mark turned to the canvas and said, "It's inspired by the farm where I work in the summer. Just over the ridge is a cliff face that drops to a rocky beach. It's a very pretty spot."

"And what secret part of you is hidden here?" Cliff asked.

Mark considered the question. "I guess it's an affinity for the ocean. The sea view wasn't part of the initial composition. It came later. The ocean is part of me. Even if I've turned my back on fishing, I still belong to the ocean." He was afraid it sounded ridiculous, but it was how he felt.

Accepting what Mark said without really understanding, Cliff admitted, "I've never stood by the ocean."

"I'll introduce you one day," Mark promised. Now out of the trance, his body asserted itself and reminded Mark of its needs. Tired and a little sore, he asked, "Could you help me clean up? I think I'm done for today."

"Sure," Cliff replied automatically.

Tidying up took longer than Cliff had thought it would. Mark carefully cleaned his brushes and tools. Cliff helped where he could, but Mark had to do most of the work. Mostly Cliff wandered the studio, examining the work of the other students. It was a kaleidoscope of subjects and styles. Cliff let them wash over him. Along one wall, a huge storage rack held dozens of canvases. Passing by it, Cliff caught a glimpse of something familiar. He stopped and very carefully pulled a painting from the rack. It was Mark.

Looking up and seeing what Cliff had found, Mark approached the big man, embarrassed. "We were required to do a self-portrait," he explained dismissively.

Cliff examined the work. In the image, Mark's face was relaxed, his eyes closed. It showed him from the shoulders up, no clothing visible. The background was dark and unresolved. The overall effect was haunting. "Why are your eyes closed?"

"I didn't want people to see me."

It made sense. Cliff understood. Privacy. Those deep dark eyes would have revealed too much. "Why do you keep it here and not at home?"

"Because I don't like it," Mark explained curtly.

"I do," Cliff stated.

"Then I may give it to you."

"Only may?" Cliff asked.

"I really don't like it," Mark admitted.

Cliff reluctantly put the painting back. "Are you ready to go?"

"Yup," Mark answered quickly.

The sun was low in the sky as they walked down Main Street. Mark offered to make supper if Cliff would help with some of the preparation. Cliff agreed, so they stopped at the store on the way to pick up a few things.

At home again, they squeezed into the tiny kitchen together. Mark prepared pasta alla carbonara as Cliff made a spinach salad. Cliff was more than a little anxious when Mark poured the raw egg mixture over the hot pasta and, after a few stirs, announced supper to be ready. He was pleasantly surprised when he tried it. The heat of the pasta cooked the eggs and created a light, creamy sauce. They chatted contentedly over the delicious supper, putting the outside world off a while longer.

The remainder of the evening passed comfortably. Cliff sat at one end of the couch, reading and making notes, while Mark curled up at the other end, studying. Occasionally, when the urge was too great, one would reach over to touch the other. Quick, casual touches of skin on skin meant to reassure and prove they were near. The desire for that contact surprised Mark. He had never felt the need before.

After a few hours of quiet reading and occasional contact, Mark decided he wanted more. Very deliberately, he set his papers on the coffee table and then crawled over to Cliff and removed the man's glasses. Placing them carefully aside, he kissed him, running a hand over Cliff's muscular frame.

Cliff laughed. "Is this my bobcat's subtle way of telling me he's horny?"

"If I say yes, will you take your clothes off?" Mark asked.

In response, Cliff got up and pulled Mark to the bedroom.

Chapter 22

It rained Thursday morning. Not a heavy downpour, but the rain was cold and penetrating. Mark usually didn't mind walking in any weather. Today, however, his injured elbow, which had only been giving him occasional minor pangs, suddenly started aching with a renewed strength. Mark wanted to go home to get a clean change of clothes. Cliff insisted on driving them. Testament to the discomfort he was experiencing, Mark agreed without argument.

The cottage felt strange to Mark. It looked the same as it had a few days before, but it felt like it belonged to someone else. In a way, it did, Mark realized. It belonged to his old self. He stepped into the bedroom. The same feeling came over him. It was strange.

Cliff helped Mark change his clothes. Mark was confident he could have managed on his own, but he enjoyed the attention. His big teddy bear appeared to take pleasure in running his hands over Mark's body, dressed or undressed. Mark had to admit he enjoyed the feel of those hands on him.

Dressed again, Mark took a few minutes to switch over the contents of his book bag. Despite the injury and the delightful distraction of suddenly and unexpectedly falling into a relationship, he had actually finished two papers. There were some notes to rewrite, a lab report to finish, and a few other minor tasks to complete, and Mark would have caught up for Monday. Not bad, he thought. He could easily have the weekend to spend with Cliff without having any homework to distract him. Pleased with the possibility, Mark placed extra socks and underwear in the bag before closing it. He looked up to find Cliff sitting on the bed, staring at the painting on the wall above

THE LAST SNOW OF WINTER

the headboard. He crawled up next to the bigger man. "What do you see?"

Cliff turned his head and kissed his lover before turning back to the image and answering. "He looks like he's waiting for someone."

"Or something," Mark suggested.

"Who is he?" Cliff asked.

"That's my friend David," Mark explained. "It looks like he could be waiting for someone. He might also be wishing for the freedom of flight. David would like to become a pilot someday." Cliff, listening quietly, nodded slowly in response. "But for me there's a special meaning."

"What's that?" Cliff asked.

"David is deeply closeted about being gay." It was one of the reasons why they couldn't work as a couple. "I think of him longing for freedom, confined to one life when secretly, he wants another."

"You and David were... together?" It was none of his business, Cliff reminded himself.

"Yes, but not successfully." Mark had been surprised they could remain friends afterward. "We needed different things. We're just friends now."

"What did you need?" Cliff asked. He wasn't sure how he knew that it was Mark who needed something different.

Mark had to admit his needs had ended their fragile relationship. David had been the one who'd said the words, but it had been Mark's needs. As they had many times before, they drove to the shore. Mark watched the ocean move like a living thing as David apologized for not being able to be what Mark needed. It didn't hurt. Though he had loved David, they hadn't been in love. "I needed to live honestly," he admitted to Cliff.

Not knowing what else to say, Cliff said, "We should get going."

Rain pelted the windows of the car as they drove without speaking. Distracted by the ache in his arm, Mark didn't notice how quiet Cliff had become. The car came to a stop near one of the entrances to the B.A.C.

"I'll pick you up later," Cliff said. "Where will you be?"

"Computer lab, as usual," Mark replied carelessly. "Until I can write again, I'll be spending a lot of time there, I think." He offered Cliff a smile. "Thanks for the drive. I'll see you later. Miss you." Mark exited the car and ran for the building.

Cliff watched him go. He even watched the door after Mark had passed through it and disappeared from sight. Finally coming to his senses, he put the car in gear and pulled away from the curb.

The gym was empty again that morning. Cliff didn't mind. He didn't feel like talking. *What am I doing with Mark? Am I being fair? Mark deserves better.* Cliff pushed himself hard into the workout. Distraction or punishment, it didn't matter. He kept pushing until his body demanded an end to the torture.

The hot water of the shower did little to relieve the pain of his muscles. He had pushed too hard and would pay for it later. Dried and dressing in the locker room, Cliff jumped when someone called his name.

"Clifford!"

The voice echoed against the hard surfaces of concrete and steel. He looked up to see Jack walking to his own locker nearby. Cliff grunted a noise in greeting. He just wasn't in the mood for this.

"Hey, Clifford, who's that guy I keep seeing you with?" Jack asked with a sneer. "He looks a little queer."

"He's a friend," Cliff responded, voice dangerously flat.

"If you say so," said Jack, apparently unconvinced.

Not wanting to lose his temper, Cliff banged his locker closed, picked up his bag, and walked out without saying anything more. *I can't do this.* He drove the route to his apartment on autopilot.

THE LAST SNOW OF WINTER

MARK worked through lunch. By early afternoon, he had finished everything pressing, even the lab report. Handwritten lab reports were the rule, but under the circumstances, he was sure the instructor would understand. Mark was delighted. He was now free to do whatever he wanted until Monday.

Every time someone opened the door to the computer room, Mark looked up, half-expecting to see Cliff. They hadn't agreed on a specific time, but if the last few days were any example, it probably wouldn't be much longer. Still, it wasn't very late. He might have an hour or so to paint if he went to the studio now. Pleased with the prospect, Mark collected his things and made for the door.

The fox painting was nearly complete. Mark paced back and forth in front of the easel. Tilting his head first one way and then the other, he considered the image. No, he finally decided, it was finished. Mark was about to put his paint and brushes away when he remembered the portrait. Technically, it was incomplete. The exercise had run so much against his grain that Mark had never really finished it. Pulling the canvas from the storage rack, he placed it on a free easel.

It isn't awful. Mark was the first to acknowledge he hadn't understood the point of doing a self-portrait, but it was required for the class. There was some lesson here he was supposed to learn. He hoped he'd learned that lesson, whatever it was. *No*, he thought, looking at the work objectively, *it isn't awful. It's just a little flat.* Mark hadn't cared for the project, and it showed. He thoughtfully squeezed little blobs of pigment onto his palette. Applying pure pigment directly to the canvas, he mixed the colors as he went. Impasto was very uncharacteristic of his usual technique, but he enjoyed the process even more for that.

Hours slipped by. Mark was unaware of the passage of time. Looking at his altered portrait, he felt ambivalence now. That was an improvement. He knew he would come to like the work in time. It might take a few days, maybe a week, but he had found something here he could appreciate. Turning his back on the image, he gathered his brushes for cleaning.

It was then, as he carefully cleaned the brushes, that Mark realized the time. It was almost seven. *Strange that Cliff hasn't come along*, Mark thought. *Then again*, he reasoned, *you didn't tell him you would be in the studio. Maybe he missed you.* Eager to see Cliff, Mark worked faster.

The sky was starless, but it wasn't raining anymore. Mark had been inside all day, so he enjoyed the cold and starless evening despite the ache in his arm and his growling stomach. He was pleased to see Cliff's car in the driveway. Light glowing from the apartment windows reassured him. He ran up the stairs and knocked but didn't wait to enter.

"Hey, Teddy Bear," Mark said cheerfully on seeing Cliff sitting on the couch.

"Hey." Cliff's response was vague, his voice uncertain.

"What's wrong?" Mark asked. "Long day?"

Cliff let out a sighing breath. "Yeah." After a few seconds, he continued by saying, "We need to talk."

Mark slipped off his coat and left his book bag next to his boots by the door. "Okay." He walked to the couch and sat down, watching the other man expectantly as he waited.

Having spent the afternoon in trying to find a good way to do this, Cliff faced the realization that there was, in fact, no good way. "I can't do this anymore," he said bluntly.

"What do you mean?" Afraid of the answer, Mark asked the question in barely a whisper.

"I can't do us. The two of us. It's not fair to you." Cliff was having trouble explaining. It made sense in his head.

"Do I get a say in this?" There was a touch of steel in Mark's voice as he said it.

"I just... I need my life to go back to the way it was." Cliff didn't want to hurt Mark. This was for the best. He deserved better than what

Cliff could offer. "You deserve someone who can be open and live honestly with you. I can't do that."

"I see. And why do you get to decide all this for me?" Mark's voice was flat, the tone reasonable.

"It's for the best." Cliff was almost pleading.

"I want you." Mark made the statement without heat but with conviction.

"I can't."

Mark stood up, putting a hand over his mouth. He paced a few times quickly and then walked to the door.

Seeing Mark pick up his coat, Cliff rose and offered, "I'll drive you home."

"No! Thank you. I'll be fine," Mark said firmly as he pulled on his boots. "Take care, Cliff." He opened the door. "I'll miss you." Remembering to grab his book bag, Mark walked out, careful not to slam the door behind him.

Cliff couldn't miss the stiff formality in Mark's voice, but he also saw light glistening on his eyes. He knew he had hurt the man. The urge to catch up to him and comfort him was strong, but Mark's manner revealed the steel of his resolve. In the face of it, Cliff hadn't dared to approach to say goodbye properly. He regretted that already.

Chapter 23

HE DIDN'T sleep. The numbers on the clock relentlessly counted the minutes as they passed. Hours dragged on, distorted beyond any reasonable semblance, and still he couldn't rest. When the numbers reached 4:30 a.m., Cliff got up. With more of the night behind him than ahead, what was the point of staying here and pretending he might fall asleep?

Cliff moved to the couch. He sat in the dark with the blind open, looking out onto the empty street. What he was looking for, he couldn't say. Maybe he was looking for something to distract his mind from reliving the last week. *Could it really have been just one week?* So much seemed to have happened, it felt like more.

Needing to remind himself why the break was for the best, Cliff reviewed the reasons for his decision. *It's for Mark's own good. He'll be better off. He needs someone else, someone who can give him more.* The reasons circled like birds, as they had for hours. The memory of Mark's face as he walked out scattered them again. *I hurt him.* Cliff closed his eyes, dropping his head to his hands.

The sky eventually grew lighter. After such a long night, Cliff half-wondered why day had bothered to come at all. Muscles sore from his workout the day before and stiff from the cold and the restless night, Cliff rose and moved to the bathroom. Hot water eased his muscles but didn't bring him any comfort. He washed mechanically. Everything reminded him of Mark. He told himself it would get easier in time. *Mark is better off.*

THE LAST SNOW OF WINTER

Following his morning routine as if nothing had changed, Cliff made a breakfast of toast and jam. He moved to the couch and sat. The flowers Mark had given him were within reach on the coffee table at his knee. The sight of the elegant buds taunted him. He turned his attention to eating, but the toast was dry and flavorless. Cliff attempted a few bites and then pushed the plate aside. He wasn't hungry.

A feeling of self-pity threatened to overwhelm him, followed by self-recrimination. *This was your own doing*, Cliff reminded himself. Whose pity did he hope to garner by calling this act a sacrifice? *You didn't give Mark up. You pushed him away.*

Cliff looked at the flowers again. They were one of the very few physical reminders of the time they'd been together. He shook his head, thinking, *Man, you've gone soft.* The flowers would stay, though. They were a gift.

Without specific plans for the day, Cliff decided it would be best to keep busy. No good would come of moping around and feeling sorry for himself. He pulled on his boots and coat and reached for the door. It was only as his hand touched the knob that it occurred to him that he might very well run into Mark. Worse, he would definitely see him in class come Monday. They had a class together Monday, Wednesday, and Friday mornings and a different class on Tuesdays and Thursdays before lunch. Forcing himself out the door, he resolved to deal with it when the time came.

Twice during the day, Cliff contemplated tracking Mark down. Just to check up on him and make sure he was okay. It didn't take much of an effort to quash the idea. There was no way Mark would want to talk to him. He was certain of that. Besides, Cliff wasn't so sure he wouldn't just beg Mark to forget the whole thing and come back.

Cliff did what he could to fill the day with activity, anything to keep his mind busy. The night, however, was another matter. As the evening turned later, the previous restless night caught up with him. Feeling overtired, he sprawled out on the bed, not even bothering to undress.

Waking disoriented, he blinked and looked at the clock. It was just after ten. Several minutes passed before he realized that he had only slept half an hour. Groaning, he rolled over and sat up. If only there was a way to know that Mark was okay.

Rising from the bed, Cliff went to the door and started getting ready to go out. He was down the stairs and heading for the street before he realized what he was doing. Halfway to Mark's cottage, he almost turned back, but the desire to know that Mark was safe was too great. He kept going.

The distance between the lamp poles grew the further he got from the downtown area. They occurred only intermittently at the edge of town. A lone streetlight stood in front of the Roselawn property. Keeping to the shadows, Cliff skirted the lit area and approached the cottage carefully. He didn't need much: a light in the window, a silhouette on the blind, anything that could prove Mark was safe and warm would satisfy Cliff. He would be disappointed, though. The blinds were open and the cottage dark. He couldn't even fool himself into believing Mark was simply asleep. It was clear that no one was home.

Cliff stood there awhile, not knowing what to do next. He turned back toward town. The realization that he might bump into Mark on his way home from campus both comforted and horrified him. *What are you doing here, anyway? Are you planning to stalk the poor guy?* Cliff walked on resolutely, keeping a wary eye ahead just in case someone might be approaching from town. Home again, he undressed and crawled into bed, prepared for a long, sleepless night.

When morning came, Cliff woke, surprised to find he'd slept after all. He didn't feel particularly rested, and his muscles ached, but he felt better than the previous morning. The memory of his visit to Mark's place the evening before caused him to flush in embarrassment. He was determined not to give in to such an impulse again. Today would be easier.

Despite the optimistic prediction, the day wasn't that much easier. Cliff had to admit it was mostly a repeat of the day before. Several times, he caught himself daydreaming. It took an effort of will to keep

THE LAST SNOW OF WINTER

busy. The distraction of returning to classes was welcome until he remembered that Mark would be there too.

Cliff was only mildly surprised to find himself standing outside Mark's cottage that afternoon. He needed to know. Approaching the door with an air of determination, he knocked sharply. The sound of someone inside gave him comfort and then filled him with apprehension. As the door opened, the feeling changed again. It wasn't Mark standing in the doorway.

A heavily built man with dark, shoulder-length hair pushed open the storm door. "Yeah?"

A surge of jealousy overcame Cliff for just a moment. He pushed it down, realizing this was probably Mark's roommate. *Besides*, part of his brain taunted viciously, *what does it matter to you anyway? You sent him away.* Collecting himself, Cliff said, "I'm looking for Mark."

"Oh. I don't think he's back yet," Jeff replied. "He'll probably be back tomorrow evening. Do you want me to give him a message?"

"No. Thanks." Cliff stepped back, away from the door. "I'll catch up with him later." Feeling deflated, Cliff took another step back and turned away. He heard the door close behind him. *Where is Mark? Maybe his roommate didn't realize Mark hadn't gone home as he'd planned. That was reasonable. Yeah, if he just got back, Jeff might not have bumped into Mark yet.* The thought lifted his spirits until Cliff remembered they weren't together anymore. He still needed to see for himself that Mark was okay.

Cliff returned to campus. The first stop would be the computer room. Mark spent a lot of time there, Cliff reasoned. Students were gradually returning to the school. There were several people working in the lab, but Mark wasn't among them. Cliff stood outside the door, feeling disappointed.

The studio was next. Certain Mark would be there, Cliff built up his confidence again. He entered the unmarked doors and walked down the quiet corridor. This area seemed unaffected by the increase in traffic elsewhere. Cliff could see the door to the studio was open, but no music filtered out. Hope sinking, he cautiously looked into the room. No one was there. He stepped in and walked to the area where Mark worked. The fox painting was still on the easel, just as it had been. In front of it, though, stood another easel. This one held Mark's portrait.

Even Cliff's untrained eye could see the change in the portrait. The image now had a depth and life to it that it didn't have before. He admired it and remembered Mark. "What have you done?" he asked himself desperately.

"Can I help you?" a voice called from somewhere.

The intrusion startled Cliff. He hadn't heard anyone come in. Turning, he saw it was Professor Robicheau. "Sorry, Professor. I was looking for Mark."

"Oh, yes. You're Mark's friend... Cliff. Yes?"

"Yes," Cliff replied.

"I'm afraid I haven't seen Mark. I was just about to lock up." The Professor indicated the door behind him. Taking the hint, Cliff walked toward the door. He passed by the other man and stepped into the hall. After carefully locking the door, Professor Robicheau turned to Cliff and said, "It was good to see you again." Cliff nodded an acknowledgement before turning and walking away.

Chapter 24

On Monday morning, Mark walked toward town mechanically. The sky was gray and the ground covered by a wet snow that had fallen through the night. Foot traffic was quickly turning the heavy snow to slush. The street was already bare. It was obvious that the snow wouldn't last the day. It was winter's swan song. Mark barely noticed. The austere whiteness held no charm today. He was thinking ahead to his second class of the day. It would be the first test. He would have to face Cliff again. Could he do it?

After leaving Cliff's apartment Thursday evening, Mark spent the sleepless night thinking over all that had happened. By morning, he was resolved to make a change. He called his parents to let them know he would be home for the weekend. He then called David.

David was annoyed at first. Annoyed by the early morning call and by the fact that Mark hadn't called sooner. To appease his friend and cut off the rant, Mark briefly sketched out some of the events of the last week. It didn't take more than that. He then asked David to meet him at the bus station in Yarmouth. David understood and readily agreed. Mark had known he would.

That evening, Mark told David everything. They sat in David's car, looking out over the ocean. Mark hadn't even needed to ask. After picking him up, David drove the car out the winding road to the lighthouse. They stayed for hours. Mark had cried unashamedly a few times while David just listened.

The weekend had been trying for Mark, but he felt better for it. He took the train back to Wolfville, arriving in town Sunday afternoon.

It hadn't been much of a vacation, but he was glad to have gone. His feet had found ground again.

Passing the duck pond, Mark couldn't help the glance up the street to where Cliff lived. He walked on quickly. His first class was in Patterson Hall on the far side of the campus.

The first period went well enough. Mark took what notes he could and arranged with a classmate to get a copy of her notes to make up for what he missed. When the class ended, he felt some apprehension over what was to come. With just enough time between his first and second class to make his way back across campus, Mark didn't have time to indulge the emotion. He collected his things and ran. Standing outside the room, Mark took a steadying breath before entering. Cliff wasn't there. Mark took his usual seat. The seat Cliff normally used was empty. *Where is he?*

Mark's next class was again on the other side of campus, this time in Elliot Hall. Classmates laughed when they found out how he'd arranged his schedule, but it was the only way Mark could fit it all in. His arts friends never seemed to understand the concept of lab periods. He had labs three afternoons a week. Painting took up the other two afternoons. That meant all his classes had to fit in the mornings. Crisscrossing the campus between periods was unavoidable.

Every now and then as Mark went about the rest of his day, he would speculate about why Cliff had been absent. It wasn't like Cliff didn't miss the odd class, especially during football season. *But why today? Was it just coincidence?* Tomorrow would tell.

The next day came. Mark felt a familiar apprehension as he approached the B.A.C. Surely Cliff would be in class this time. Mark took his seat. Tables formed a large, open rectangle with chairs arranged around the perimeter. Cliff normally sat directly opposite Mark on the other side of the room, but again his seat was empty. *What happened?*

When Wednesday's class was a repeat of Monday, Mark became concerned. *Why isn't Cliff coming to class? Should I go find him?* No, he couldn't do that. *What, then?* During chemistry, Mark decided what he would do.

Skipping lunch, Mark ran to the building where he knew most of the psychology professors had their offices. The directory inside the door guided him to Dr. Hansen's office. The door was open. Mark knocked on the jamb quickly before he could reconsider.

When Dr. Hansen looked up, it took him just a moment to recognize Mark. When he did, he smiled warmly. "Mark, what can I do for you?"

Not certain how to proceed, Mark asked cautiously, "Have you spoken with Cliff recently?"

That's an odd way to start a conversation, the professor thought. "Not since last week. Is everything all right?"

"We've... we're not together." Mark explained clumsily. "He hasn't been to class, and I just wanted to know that he was... okay."

Dr. Hansen considered the information. "I haven't seen him, but we have a meeting scheduled for tomorrow morning. If he doesn't show, I'll check up on him."

"Thank you," Mark said. It was something.

As Mark turned to go, Dr Hansen spoke to him again. "I'm very sorry things didn't work out between you two."

"So am I." Saying the words filled Mark with sadness at what he had lost. Unable to say more, he waved goodbye to Dr. Hansen and walked away quickly.

WHEN Thursday morning came, Cliff forced himself out of bed. He had been making excuses to his professors about missing classes. This morning, though, he had a meeting with his mentor. He needed to get off his ass and get back out there. Showered and shaved for the first time in days, he left his apartment and headed to Dr. Hansen's office.

The door was open, as it usually was when Ted was at work. Cliff knocked on the frame to announce himself, waiting only a moment before walking in and sitting down.

Dr. Hansen studied his student carefully. "Good morning, Cliff," he said lightly. "You're not looking like your usual self. Is everything all right?"

Cliff considered evading. He didn't want to talk about Mark. Not even with his mentor.

"Before you answer," Ted explained as he got up and tactfully closed the door, "I should tell you that Mark came by yesterday asking about you."

"What did he say?" Cliff asked uneasily.

"He said you two were no longer together." Ted sat down again and observed his friend. "He's worried about you. He said you've missed classes."

"I wasn't ready to face him again," Cliff confessed.

That was a surprise. Dr. Hansen was certain there were few things that would intimidate Cliff. "Do you want to talk about it?"

Cliff considered the offer to share. *Do I want to talk about it? No,* he assessed honestly. *But maybe it will help.* Cliff breathed out, "I think I've made a horrible mistake." Once he started, it was easier to continue. He told Ted everything. It was a relief to let it all go.

After listening to his friend and student pour out his heart, Ted considered what he could say. It sounded like Cliff already had his answers and just needed a little gentle push. "So you decided Mark needed someone who was out?"

"Because I wasn't out, I couldn't be honest about our relationship," Cliff explained. "It wouldn't have been fair to him."

"Do you think the fear of being outed, yourself, played a part in your decision?" Ted prodded gently.

"Yeah, I think so." Cliff had to be honest.

THE LAST SNOW OF WINTER

"And you feel you've made a mistake?"

"Yeah," Cliff answered quietly.

"How so?"

That very question had been playing on his mind for the last few days. Cliff replied, "If I could go back in time, I think I would rather risk being outed than be without Mark."

Ted leaned forward and put a hand on Cliff's arm. "You can't go back, but you could talk to him."

The suggestion stunned Cliff. "I hurt him."

Nodding his head in agreement, Ted said, "That may be. But I think he would be willing to listen." Looking to his watch, Dr. Hansen laughed humorlessly. "Your love life is really eating into our professional relationship. We will need to reschedule this meeting yet again. I'm sorry. I really have to go." He rose and put a hand on the big man's shoulder. "Talk to him."

There was still time before class. Cliff decided to go to the gym. A workout might help him focus his mind. It sounded odd to some, but the gym usually helped Cliff relax. Unlike last week, the weight room wasn't empty this morning. Cliff met up with Tony, a teammate, and they took turns spotting each other on the bench press.

It was during a set of repetitions that Jack walked by and asked loudly, "Hey Clifford, where's your boyfriend? I haven't seen you guys around."

Tony answered. "What's wrong, Jack-off? You jealous, or are you looking to get hooked up?"

"Fuck you!" Jack stalked off in the direction he had been heading.

Cliff pushed the bar up one last time, dropping it heavily in its cradle. He sat up and then got to his feet angrily. Without even thanking Tony for spotting, he headed for the showers.

"Hey, Cliff, wait up," Tony called after him. When he caught up, he said, "You know you shouldn't let Jack-off get to you. He's an asshole."

Cliff almost snarled. "What if he's right?" He gave Tony a grim look that lasted for a few seconds, daring him to say something, and then turned for the shower room again.

Tony followed him. He said quietly, "Fuck, Cliff. Are you serious?"

Cliff stopped. Pinching the bridge of his nose and closing his eyes, he replied flatly, "I'm gay."

"Look, Cliff, if you dig guys... well hey, that's your business." Tony kept his voice confidential. "But you know some of these guys here are going to give you grief. Fuck, are you sure about this?"

Turning quickly to face Tony, Cliff barked, "Does this sound like something I'm going to joke about?"

"Hey, don't take my head off. I'm your friend." Tony held his palms up toward Cliff as a sign of surrender.

"I'm sorry, Tony," said Cliff. "I'm just having a hard time with this."

Tony gave the other man a friendly if somewhat solid slap across the backside. "So are you going to become a decorator?"

"Yeah, asshole. Have you seen my apartment?" They laughed at the joke, which broke the tension. "Thanks, Tony."

"You're welcome. Now keep your eyes to yourself while I shower," Tony requested, mock serious.

"Don't worry," Cliff replied. "You don't have anything I want."

Tony's easy acceptance of Cliff's confession surprised him. The guy was hetero to the max. On the other hand, he was a decent guy. Cliff was beginning to think that maybe he should give people the opportunity to surprise him. One person in particular came to mind.

Chapter 25

MARK arrived just barely in time for class. His first physio session had been earlier that morning at the clinic. To call the experience an ordeal would be an understatement. Mark was convinced the physiotherapist was secretly a sadist who had been fortunate enough to find an ideal line of work. However, she assured him that, given time, the process would help restore his arm's strength and range of motion. Right then, though, Mark's arm ached miserably.

Taking his usual seat, Mark was disappointed but not entirely surprised to see that Cliff's was still empty. He pulled out a notebook in preparation for class. With all the practice, he was getting pretty good at taking notes with his left hand. Distracted by digging through his bag for a pen, Mark was startled when someone spoke to him from just over his shoulder.

"Could we talk after class?"

Mark was stunned. It was Cliff. He stood close by, leaning forward to bring his mouth close to Mark's ear. His voice was quiet, but the tone was insistent. So taken aback by the request and the sudden reappearance of his former lover, Mark could only nod in reply. Satisfied, Cliff straightened and moved to his regular spot on the other side of the room. Mark watched him go, wondering what he could want to discuss.

The professor entered and started the day's lesson without preamble. Mark tried to follow, but his mind and eye kept wandering to the man sitting opposite. Cliff seemed to be studiously keeping his attention toward the front of the room. He wasn't wearing his public face, Mark noticed, but he still couldn't guess what was on the big guy's mind.

Thinking that the last eighty-five minutes must have been the longest on record, Mark was relieved when the class finally ended. He quickly collected his things. Looking up to scan the room, he found Cliff standing nearby as if to make sure Mark wouldn't try to slip away. Without exchanging a word, Mark fell into step beside him, and they exited the room together.

Safe in the artificial privacy of the crowd of students moving around them, Cliff said, "I'm on lunch. Do you have a little time?"

"I have painting now," Mark admitted. Seeing the look of disappointment on the other man's face, he conceded. "The class is very casual. I can talk for a few minutes. Come on." Together they took the door that led to the studio wing. Walking past the studio, Mark stopped partway down the empty hall and turned to the other man expectantly.

Cliff took a deep breath. "You must be angry with me."

Had he made a guess at what Cliff was going to say, that statement wouldn't have been it at all. He thought about it and carefully framed his reply. "I was angry for a while. But no, I'm not angry with you." He waited for more. The pause grew, but Cliff seemed no closer to sharing whatever it was he had wanted to say. Not in a humor to prolong this torture, Mark prodded, "What did you want to talk to me about?"

Stirred out of inaction by the tone of irritation as much as by the question, Cliff said immediately, "I wanted to apologize."

A confused clatter interrupted them. Mark interpreted the sound: his classmates heading for the studio. To spare Cliff any embarrassment, Mark motioned silently that he should follow. They moved further along the hallway, away from the noise. The hallway ended at a door that opened onto a rarely used stairwell. Mark pushed past the door with Cliff a step behind him. The latch clicked loudly and the metal door banged back into place, closing off the voices from the

THE LAST SNOW OF WINTER

hall. Turning to Cliff again, he said, "I accept your apology." His voice echoed hollowly in the tall space.

"Do you think you could ever forgive me?" Cliff asked.

"I already have." Mark shrugged.

"Really," Cliff said without thinking. "Why?"

What could Mark say? "We all have to do things in our own time." It had been surprisingly easy to forgive Cliff. Perhaps it was the guilt he felt at walking out that had made it easy. "I should have stayed and talked it through." It was probably better he hadn't, but he owed Cliff that much. "Besides, I still love you." *Maybe that wasn't the best thing to say*, Mark realized as he said it.

Swallowing past a lump in his throat, Cliff confessed hoarsely, "I was scared."

"What scared you?" Mark asked the question, surprised that Cliff had been able to make the admission.

Cliff had been thinking about it for days. "Things were changing so fast. My life was changing. It felt like I was losing control of everything. It was all getting out of hand. And then I was afraid I would hurt you."

Mark creased his brow and narrowed his eyes. "I don't understand."

Dropping his head and taking a step closer, Cliff tried to explain. "Our time together was fantastic, a daydream made real. But come Monday, I would've needed to pretend again. It wouldn't have been fair to you. I would have hurt you and then lost you." Cliff shook his head angrily. "It makes sense in my head. I'm just not explaining very well."

"I think I understand." Objectively, Mark believed he could appreciate the situation Cliff had found himself in. "I really should be going." He made a move for the door.

Cliff held out his hand as if to reach for the other man. "Wait." He carefully refrained from touching Mark uninvited.

Mark stopped and waited, still facing the door.

"Is there any chance we could... fix this?" Cliff spoke the last two words in a hushed voice.

Mark heard the question. It wasn't hard to admit that he wanted to say yes. He turned back to face the big man and sighed. "Look, Cliff, I can't say I'm not tempted, but things have changed." Pausing just long enough to take a breath, Mark continued. "I came out to my parents last weekend. I'm done pretending. I'm now officially and completely out." The announcement to his parents had been difficult for Mark to make and even harder for them to hear. Their relationship wasn't yet out of the woods, but Mark hoped the situation would improve in time. He watched Cliff closely to see his reaction. "Maybe you were right. It was probably only a matter of time before things fell apart. I do need to live honestly."

"What if I want the same thing?" Cliff said simply.

Too shocked to speak, Mark could only blink.

Impatient for more of a reaction, Cliff asked, "You don't believe me?"

"Do you mean it?" Mark's voice sounded small in his own ears.

Cliff pulled Mark close. "Would you take me back? Out in the open for everyone to see?"

Voice shaky, almost overcome with emotion, Mark answered, "Yes. Yes, of course I would, you big moose."

Overjoyed, Cliff held Mark too tightly and kissed him hungrily. He was distantly aware of a familiar noise from somewhere overhead. The bang and click of a door opening and the sound of footsteps rattling down the stairs echoed unheeded in the air around them. Their intrusion wasn't enough to make Cliff want to let go. The footsteps stopped abruptly as if in surprise.

"Gentlemen! In the stairwell?" The speaker sounded amused.

Cliff loosened his hold on Mark and turned boldly to face the person who had addressed them.

"Oh Mark," said Professor Robicheau, unembarrassed, "I didn't see you there." He added casually, "I'll be starting a round of critique in about twenty minutes. Nice to see you again, Cliff." He descended the last few steps, pulled open the door, and left the stairwell, humming as if nothing at all unusual had happened.

"What?" Cliff asked, looking to Mark with a bewildered expression.

"He's telling me I still have a few minutes to be with my boyfriend before I have to get to class," Mark interpreted happily. "As I said, it's pretty laid-back around here." He stroked Cliff's face with his left hand. "I missed this fuzzy face."

They kissed again.

"Are you really sure about this? What about your career?" Mark asked uneasily.

Cliff stole another kiss before responding. "Careers change." When Mark only gave him a quizzical look, he clarified, "It just wasn't happening. I'm in my fifth year of a four year program. I took an extra year to give it one more shot. It's time to face facts. I'm not going to play football professionally. I'm not my brother."

The assertion stunned Mark. They would need to talk about that later. "So what will you do?"

"I'll start my masters degree. Dr. Hansen has offered to help." The prospect made Cliff nervous, but it was exciting too. It also presented some obstacles to their potentially on-again relationship. "If I'm lucky, I'll be able to get into Dal this fall." The realities of a long distance relationship might cool their reunion, he realized. Mark's only reaction was to give him a sly smile. "What?" Cliff knew something was up.

"I didn't tell you. I've applied to NSCAD." Mark was smiling broadly now.

"What's that?" Cliff asked.

"The Nova Scotia College of Art and Design," he explained. "Funny thing, it's not far from Dalhousie."

Stunned at first and then overjoyed, Cliff hugged Mark tightly. He lifted the smaller man and swung him around. He let go when he heard Mark grunt in pain. "Sorry. I couldn't help myself." After a heartbeat, he asked, "So what happens now, Bobcat?"

"Well, Teddy Bear, why don't we have dinner tonight and talk about it," replied Mark. Remembering his class, he said, "I really should get going."

They walked back to the studio together. On reaching the door, Mark turned to say goodbye, but Cliff surprised him by pulling him into a hug and kissing him goodbye instead. Released again, Mark turned toward the open door of the studio. It seemed only two of his classmates had caught the show. One turned away self-consciously while the other just looked on, wearing an expression of shock.

"Is this what I'm going to have to put up with?" Mark asked with a laugh as he pulled Cliff out of the line of sight of the studio.

"Yes," admitted Cliff cheerfully. "But it's too late now. You already agreed."

"I'm glad you came back," Mark said soberly.

"Who else would take me?" Cliff asked. "Can I come by after class to get you?"

"Yeah," Mark agreed. "And if you behave yourself, I'll introduce you to some people."

"That sounds like a challenge," Cliff toyed. He turned to go. "Love you."

"Get going, you big moose," Mark said in response. "Love you too."

When it comes down to it, IAN MUISE would probably be reluctant to call himself a writer. Instead, he likes to think of himself as simply playing host to the party of characters who live inside his head. And like any good host, he is happy to make the introductions, then stand back and discreetly watch the story unfold. The idea of narrating those stories is a new phenomenon, brought on in part by the encouragement and support of the most amazingly patient husband a man could ever ask for.

Ian and said husband live in a small town on the east coast of Canada together with their two cats, excellent paperweights both. He hopes to continue telling the stories of the people he meets in his head.

Contemporary Romance from DREAMSPINNER PRESS

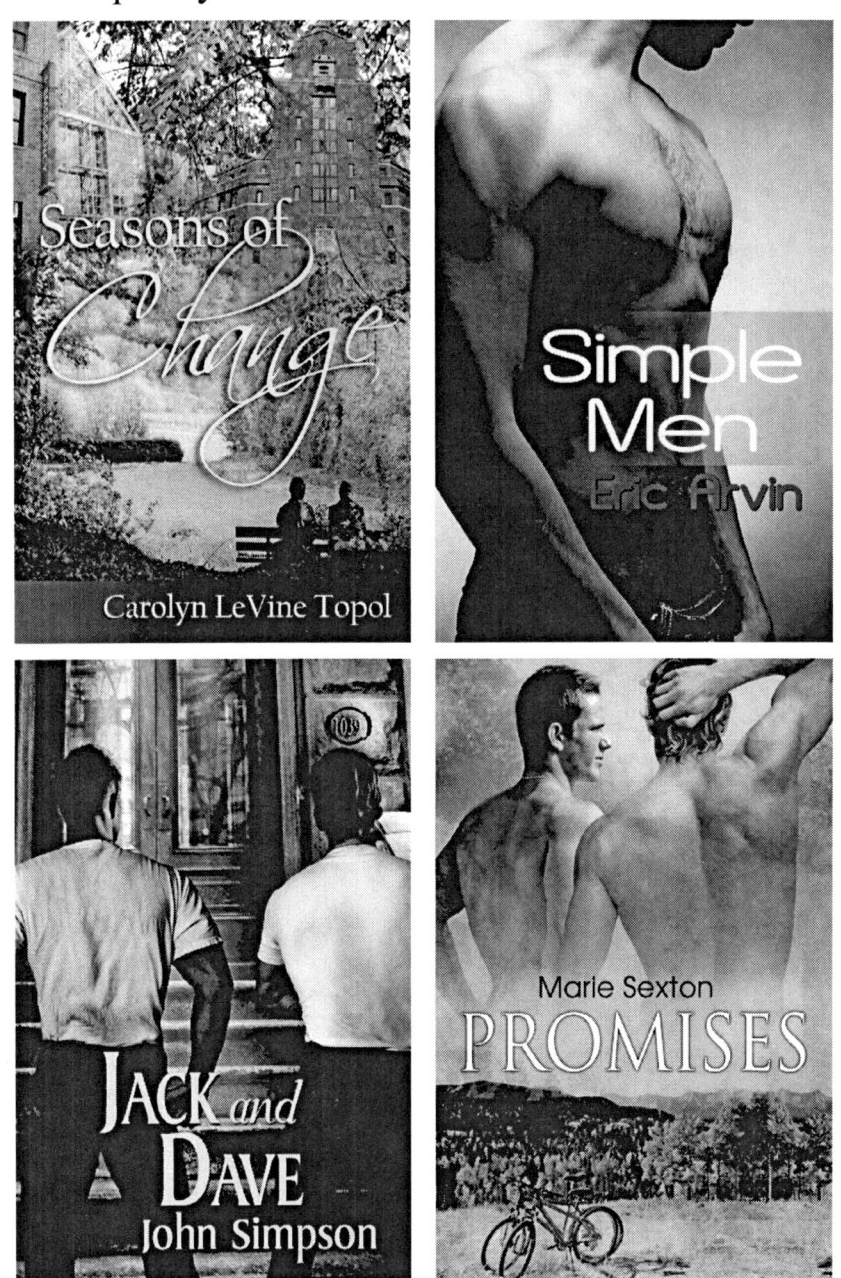

http://www.dreamspinnerpress.com

Dreamspinner Press
For more of the
best M/M romance,
visit
Dreamspinner Press
www.dreamspinnerpress.com